호모 스토리우스

호모 스토리우스

신 훈 시집

Homo storious
The human species with stories

좋은땅

머리글

사라져가지만 기억해야하는 것들
잊혀져가지만 되돌리고 싶은 것들
소멸되어가지만 잡아둬야 하는 것들
퇴색되어가지만 미련이 남는 것들
떠나가지만 간직해야 하는 것들.

그런 것들을 남겨두는 것은 글을 쓰는 것이었다.
삶의 순간순간 틈새를 타고 올라오는 감정과 생각을 썼다.
누군가 한 사람이라도 공감하고 위로받길 바라는 마음이 크고,
재미를 느낀다면 더욱 감사한 일이다.

슬픈 이야기든, 즐거운 이야기든 우리들 모두는 이야기를 품고 사는
호모 스토리우스다.

목차

교통사고

주차된 차의 범퍼를 갈고 간 사람이 차에서 내려 여기저기 살펴보고 있다
새끼를 동반한 어미새다
안절부절못하면서 실수를 인정하고
보상금을 드리겠다는 그 표정과 말투에 난처함만 가득하다
덩달아 그 딸린 새끼도 안절부절못하니 오히려 이들을 보호해야 할 것만 같다
범퍼야 원래 부딪히는 용도니 신경 쓰지 마시고 그냥 가셔도 된다고 쿨하게
보내드리고 생각했다

바보 같은 놈!

Traffic Accident

A person who scratched the bumper of a parked car gets out of the car and is looking around.

It's a mother bird with her baby bird.

Her facial expression and tone of voice are filled with helplessness as she admits her mistake, offers compensation while being restless.

At the same time, the baby birds are also restless rather I feel like they need to be protected.

I said without hesitation, "Car bumpers are meant to be bumped, so don't worry, you can just go." and thought,

'I'm such a fool!'

소심남의 잠자리

초집적 반도체를 만들어내듯
내 마음도 몹시 정교하고 빈틈이 없다고… 없다고…
자신하며 자위하고 삽니다
그래야 걱정을 내려놓을 수 있으려나요
일도 관계도 그렇게 마음 쓰며 하루를 마칩니다
부딪히는 사람들도 생각들이 있겠지만 세심한 계산 속에
별일 아님을 결론짓고 잠자리에 듭니다

A timid man's bed

Just like creating ultra-integrated semiconductors, also my mind is extremely
sophisticated and
I live consoling myself with the assurance there are no gaps in my mind.
Is that how I can let go of my worries?
I end the day with so much thought in my work and relationships.
Everyone who bumps into me may have thoughts, but after careful
calculations,
I conclude it's no big deal and go to bed.

전염병

좁은 공간에서 서로의 숨이 섞인 공기를 나누기 싫어 숨을 참았다
길거리에서조차도 서로의 숨을 피해 다녔다
사람이 사람을 경계하고 혐오하던 삭막한 시절
중세에서나 가능했을 인도대륙에서 드러난 히말라야 산맥을 보며 인류는 큰
죄악을 절감했었다
탐욕과 파괴를 문명의 진보라고 우기던 이들도 숙연했었다
공포의 바이러스가 약해지고 사람들도 적응해간 3년의 세월
사람들은 얼마나 변했을까?
나에게도 변화가 찾아왔는가?

Contagion

We held our breath, not wanting to share the air with each other's breath in the cramped space.

Even on the street, we avoided each other's breath.

A desolate time when people were wary and loathed others.

Seeing the Himalayan Mountains revealed in the Indian continent, which would have been possible only in the Middle Ages, mankind felt a great sense of sin.

Even those who insisted that greed and destruction were the progress of civilization were solemn.

3 years have passed since the virus of fear weakened and people adapted, how much have people changed?

Has change come to me too?

휴일

일요일 아침
길가의 비둘기도 한가롭고
차들도 드물게 지나는 이면도로가 커피숍에서
다시 마주한 나 자신
꺼칠한 수염, 떡 진 머리

Day off

On sunday morning

I met myself again at a coffee shop on a side road where the pigeons were

quiet and cars rarely passed by

had a rough beard, greasy hair

자연

해가 의례히 비추고
비가 때 되면 내리는
그냥 그렇게 하릴없음에 깃든 자연의 힘

Nature

The sun shines habitually,

rain falls when the time comes,

the power of nature in the dwelling in nothingness

대지

때로는 자전거를 타는 것조차 방자하게 느껴져서
두 발을 땅에 디디고 걷는다
지구별에 하나의 생명으로 잠시 머물다 스러지는 찰나의 존재가
이 땅에 발 딛고 서서 걷는 원초적 경배

Earth

Sometimes, even riding a bike feels self-indulgent, so I walk with feet on
the ground
The primal worship of fleeting being that stays on Earth as a life for a while
and then passes away

시골의 달

내가 나고 자란 시골의 달은 몹시도 외롭고 황량했다
기껏해야 보름달빛이 약간의 푸근함을 주었을까
그 달은 어디서나 같았을 테지만
그 시골 깡촌의 달은 그냥 서글펐다

The moon of countryside

The moon of countryside where I was born and raised
was extremely lonely and desolate.
At most, did the full moonlight give a little warmth?
The moon would have been the same everywhere
but the moon in that rural village was just sad.

무기

저 압정은 외계인 방어용
지구에 쉬이 내리다가는 가는 수가 있다는 무서운 무기
아, 생각만 해도 안전해

Weapon

Those thumb-tacks are for alien defense

A scary weapon that can easily kill them if they just drop it on the Earth.

Oh, it's safe just to think about it

생명의 반대말

사람이 외로워서 죽는다
외로워서 병을 키우고
외로워서 거칠게 살며
명을 단축시키고자 무던히 노력한다
외로움은 생명의 반대말이다

The opposite word of life

People die because they are lonely
People get sick because they are lonely
People live roughly because they are lonely
And people try hard to shorten their life.
Loneliness is the opposite of life

엇나간 자식을 둔 부모에게 주는 위로

고통스럽고
헤어날 길 보이지 않고
삶이 원래 이런 건가 신물이 나고
할 수 있는 역할조차도 없이 무력해도

폭풍이 치고 서리가 내려 앙상한 가지에
푸른 이파리는 꿈도 꾸지 못하는 세월이어도

부지런한 농부처럼 묵묵히 살아내다 보면
따사로운 햇볕 드는 날들이 쌓이다 보면

시간은 흐르고
인연은 섞이며
바람이 불어서

사람도 철이 들고
나뭇가지에 연두색 새잎이 난다

고통의 시간만큼 주름은 깊게 파여도
결국 봄날도 오고 웃을 날도 오는 세상 이치

Consolation to parents whose children have gone astray

Distressing and
I can not see a way out
sick and tired of wondering
if life is really like this
even though I'm powerless without any role I can

Even when storms, frost fall
so green leaves cannot even dream of bare branches

If you live quietly like a diligent farmer
as warm sunny days pile up day by day,

time goes by
relationship is mixed
the wind blows

people are mature
new green leaves grow on branches

Even if the wrinkles become
as deep as the time of pain,
that's the way the cookie crumbles eventually spring will come and days
when we can smile will also come.

자본주의

안정된 수입이 사람을 안정시킨다
행복의 근원으로까지 올라간다
자본주의를 욕하지 마라
태어난 이상 사냥은 생존이다
한겨울 육고기를 잡아야 먹고 입고 번식도 가능하다
자본주의는 인간 삶의 원형이다
아! 밥 멕여 주는 사회주의가 좋다

Capitalism

Stable income makes people stable

and increases the source of happiness

Don't criticize capitalism

Since you were born, hunting is survival.

It's possible to eat, wear, and reproduce only by catching meat in the middle

of winter.

Capitalism is the archetype of human life.

Ah! I like socialism that feeds people

올챙이

꼬물꼬물 일하고
꼬물꼬물 사고 치며
꼬물꼬물 해결하면서
꼬물꼬물 울며불며
꼬물꼬물 시끄럽게 떠들기도 하면서
사람들이 살아갑니다
저 높이 조금 먼 하늘에서 보면 말입니다

Tadpole

People live working wriggle wriggle like a tadpole,

making troubles wriggle wriggle,

solving them wriggle wriggle,

crying and complaining wriggle wriggle,

chattering loudly wriggle wriggle

If you look at it from a little high up in the sky

도시

희로애락 애오욕
칠정이 넘실대는 도시
숙소 같은 집에서 눈 붙이고, 전쟁터 같은 직장으로
쳇바퀴 도는 일상
해는 뜨고 지고

City

A city overflowing with
7 emotions(joy, anger, sorrow, pleasure, love, hatred and desire)
sleep for a moment at a house that feels like an accommodation then go to
a workplace like the battlefield
Daily life repeats a routine endlessly
the sun rises and sets

50대 아저씨

털 같은 약한 뿌리만 물속에 담그고
물만 먹고 버티는 부초처럼
50대 아저씨는 늙어간다

Man in his 50s

Like a floating grass that survives by submerging only its weak, hair-like
roots in water and drinking only water
A man in his 50s gets old like that.

고독

꼬리표가 아니라 본질이다
아닌 척, 모르는 척 살고 싶지만
중심에 떠억 자리 잡은 쇠기둥이다

Loneliness

It's not a label but nature
we want to live pretending not to be or not to know
but it's a steel pillar located in front of the center

자식과 어머니

무너지고 흩어져서 사라지고 싶어도
그러지 못하게 부여잡는 존재가 있다
자식…
어머니…

자식이 없었다면
어머니가 일찍 돌아가셨다면
미련도 없는 팍팍한 삶
아마도 필시 거칠게 내달렸을 것이다

Children and mother

Even if somebody wants to fall apart, scatter and disappear
there are beings who hold to prevent from doing so
children…
mothers…

If there were no children
or mother died early on
A tough life with no motivation to live
most likely ran through roughly

얼음행성

서로의 온기로 버텨내고 지켜내는 삶
지구는 혼자 살기에 적합한 행성이 아니다

An ice planet

The life that endures and protects with each other's warmth
Earth is no longer a suitable planet for living alone.

눈이 내린 아침

눈이 허벅지만큼 쌓인 날
어머니는 새벽밥을 짓느라 아궁이에 생솔가지 불 지피며
하얀 연기에 눈물, 콧물 씨름하신다

툇마루 아래 누렁이와 새끼들은 새어 나온 연기에 같이 깽깽거리고

무거운 솜이불 속 단잠을 부여잡느라
눈 치우라는 어머니 고함이 야속하다

세상이 하얗고 굴뚝 연기도 하얀 날 아침
그 시절 시간은 참 더디 갔다

Snowy morning

A day when there's snow on the ground as high as thighs
mother stokes raw pine branches in the furnace to make an early breakfast
struggling with her tears and runny nose for the white smoke

Yellowy and her cubs under the Toenmaru(Korean traditional veranda)
yipped together in the smoke that had leaked out

I was trying to catch a sound sleep under my thick cotton blanket
it sounded badly for mother's yell to shovel the snow

But on a morning when the world and smoke of chimney was white
in those days, time went by very slowly

무제 1

개미나 사람이나
그게 그거

Untitled 1

There's little difference between the ants and people

그리다

우리는 무언가를 그리며 살아갑니다
그리는 마음이 우리를 어딘가로 이끌어 갑니다

성취든 보고픔이든 사랑이든
복수나 저주를 그리는 마음조차
교차하고 섞이며 세상이 돌아갑니다

당신은 무엇을 그립니까?

Miss

We live with longing.
The heart that longs for leads us somewhere

Whether it's achievement, missing or love

Even thoughts of revenge or curses are running through our mind and mixing to run the world

What are you miss…?

휴식

하릴없음과
침묵과
무심한 햇볕과 바람이
영혼을 자유롭게 합니다

Taking a break

With nothing to do
and silence,
the indifferent sunlight and wind
sets the soul free

하루의 끝

늦은 밤
인식의 촉수는 무뎌지고
곤함으로 몸이 늘어진다
독하게 피어나던 감정도
불 꺼진 숯이 되었다
자자… 다 부질없다

End of the day

Late at night
the tentacles of perception become dull,
body goes limp from fatigue,
and the emotions that were blooming strongly
became like charcoal that had gone out
let's just sleep… it's all futile.

4월 어드메쯤

햇볕이 제법 사람을 괴롭힐 만하오
나무의 새순이야 연두색으로 신난 듯하나
사람이 봄이라고 특히 자라는 것도 아닌데
왜 이렇게 싱숭생숭한 건지

Sometime in April

The sunlight can bother people quite a bit
tree's sprout are light green and look excited,
but people don't grow particularly in spring
why is our mind so cluttered

삶의 터전

출퇴근하는 거리
걸어서 다니는 술집 밥집
장 보고 학원 다니는 길들

보고 듣고 냄새를 맡고
뜨는 해 지는 해 바라보며
살아가는 동네

Living foundation

Street commuting to work
Bars and restaurants we go to on foot
Streets where we come and go while shopping for groceries or going to
academy

The town where we live,
see, hear and smell
looking at the rising and setting sun.

운명

지나고 보면 갈 길 간 거
지나고 나니 알게 된 거
사람들은 운명이라고 하고 나도 그렇게 체념한다
언어의 마술인지 시간의 마술인지
그렇게 사람들은 수긍하고 산다

Destiny

In hindsight, people say they have gone their own way
they have found out later
People say it's fate and I'm resigned to that, too
If it's the magic of language or the magic of time, but
that's how people accept and live.

당신의 의미

일하기 싫은 마음이 생겨도
지쳐 쉬고 싶기만 해도
나는 생각 없는 기계라고 되뇌며 버팁니다

기계가 잠시 숨을 쉬며 사람이 되는 순간
당신!

Your meaning

Even if I don't want to work
even if I'm tired and just want to rest
I hold on to myself by telling 'I'm a mindless machine'

When a machine takes a moment to breathe and becomes a human,
That's you!

구원

주말 빨간 날
내 영혼을 돌보는 날
주중이 되면 다시금 피폐해지고
반복되는 일상

나에게 구원은 있는가?

Redemption

Weekend the red day

It is a day to take care of my soul.

But during the week, I become exhausted again.

It's a repetitive my daily life

Is there redemption for me?

롱스커트를 입은 여인

걸을 때마다 다리 윤곽이 천 위에 드러나는
롱스커트를 입은 여인은 참 아름답다
과하지도 부족하지도 않은 드러남 속에 숨겨진
그녀의 힘과 절제가 아름답다
알되 다 알지 못하고, 열심이되 자랑할 것 없다고 사는 사람의
겸양도 롱스커트를 입은 여인 같다

A woman wearing a long skirt

A woman wearing a long skirt that shows the outline of her legs on the
fabric every time she walks is very beautiful.

Her strength and restraint hidden in a revealing that is neither too much nor
too little is beautiful.

The humbleness of a person who knows but does not know everything,
and lives with enthusiasm but nothing to boast about, is also like a woman
wearing a long skirt.

미니스커트

시원하게 드러낸 다리
있는 그대로 거리낌 없는 자유
일체의 부정과 편견도 없는 자연의 상태
수군대고 훔쳐보는 년놈이 죄인이다

Mini skirt

Cool exposed legs

Freedom as it is without hesitation

A state of nature without any negativity or prejudice

The bad ass bitches and guys who whisper about it and peep at are sinners.

장마

십 일 동안 비가 온댄다
지상에 살지만 반물고기가 되어야 할 판이다
공기 중 습도는 80프로
쿠팡에서는 인공 아가미를 팔 것이다
수영하는 마음으로 출근길 걸으며
젖은 바지를 끌고 구명보트 같은 사무실에 안착했다

The rainy season

They said it would rain for 10 days.

Even though I live on land but I have to be half a fish.

The humidity in the air is as high as 80%.

Coupang site should sell artificial gills

Walking to work with the mind of swimming

I landed safely in an office that felt like a lifeboat, dragging my wet pants.

소

자칭 '소'라는 여자가 있다
스스로 순하고 순종적이며 묵묵히 나아가는 소 같은 여자라고 한다

나는 늘 소를 좋아했다
그래서 그 여자가 소 같다고 하니 새삼 예뻐 보였다

그런데 그 여자는 한마디를 덧붙였다
순한 소가 화나면 그땐 뵈는 게 없다고

Cow

There is a woman who calls herself 'cow'
She calls herself a cow-like woman who is docile, obedient, and moves
forward silently.
I always liked cows
So when she said she looked like a cow, she looked pretty again.
But the woman added one saying
: When a obedient cow gets angry, it can get even angrier without seeing
anything.

전장

나는 사무실에 출근하여 일이 한가한 시간에
독서도 하고 뜨개질도 하려고 시도해 봤지만 손에 잡히지 않았었다

그 이유가 몹시 궁금하던 차에
전장의 병사와 양복 입은 내 모습이 겹치면서
그 이유를 알게 되었다

그래, 적군의 공격을 하염없이 기다리는 병사는
쉬고 있는 상태가 아니었어

내가 그 병사였어!

Battleground

When I went to the office

I tried reading and knitting during my free time, but I couldn't get my hands on it.

At the moment when I was very curious about the reason, the image of a soldier on the battleground and myself wearing a suit overlapped, and I realized the reason.

That's right, the soldier waiting endlessly for the enemy's attack was not resting at all.

I was that soldier!

관조

지나는 사람들을 바라보고
길가에 풀들과 줄지어 가는 개미들도 바라본다

가족들의 표정을 바라보고
일하는 직원들의 모습도 바라본다

비 내리는 하늘과
해 지고 떠오르는 달과 별을 바라본다

도시 저 너머 어렴풋한 산도 바라본다
세상을 바라본다.

바라봄이 멈추는 그 순간까지
나는 많은 것들을 바라보며 살겠지

Looking at

I look at the people passing by, the grass on the side of the road, and the ants lined up.

I look at the expressions of my family and the employees at work.

I look at the rainy sky, the moon and stars as the sun sets and rises.

I look at the vague mountains beyond the city. And also I look at the world.

Until the moment I stop looking, I will live looking at many things

출가

나이 60줄에 머리 깎고 출가한 형
뭘 버릴 게 있다고 출가까지 하는지

이등병도 쓴다는 핸드폰이라서 그런지
행자승도 쓰더라

복날 삼계탕은 못 먹어도 계란 두 알 챙겼다고
자랑인지 푸념인지
검은 비닐봉지에 고이 모신 계란 사진

형의 농 속의 치열함을 달래주고 싶어
마시던 캔맥주 사진 전송

'마구니를 넘어서시옵소서'
글과 함께…

Becoming a buddhist monk

My older brother, who shaved hair and became a monk when he was almost 60 years old, and I'm wondering what he has to throw away

Maybe it's because a cell phone used by a private
even Buddhist monk uses that kind of cell phone, too.

Even on days when he was supposed to eat health food, my older brother couldn't eat Samgyetang(Ginseng Chicken Soup), but he took 2 eggs. whether he was bragging or complaining, he sent me a photo that he treasured the eggs in a black plastic bag

In my older brother's joke, I wanted to ease his life in the fast lane so I sent him a picture of the can of beer
with the words 'Please overcome the Devil'…

시작

할아버지 할머니도 젊게 맹그는 마법
시작!
사랑을 하든 못자리를 파든
시작해 봅시다
시작은 살아있는 자의 전유물
뭘 시작하든 바로 젊음으로 돌아갑니다

The beginning

The magic that makes even grandparents young is
the beginning!
Whether in love or digging a grave
It's time to get started
The beginning is the exclusive property of living people
Whatever you begin doing, you'll go right back to youth.

성장

몸이 아프면 마음은 성장한다
세상일은 접어두고
자신의 몸과 마음에 깊이 침잠하기 때문이리라

혈기왕성한
우리 집 사춘기 딸들은 도무지 아프지 않는다
아빠의 인사에도 대답하지 않을 만큼
오만방자하다

아빠는 자기수양을 위해
일주일에도 몇 번씩 숙취를 불러들여 정진하고 있거늘

Growth

After the body sicks, the mind grows

Leave the world behind

It may be because you sink deeply into your own body and mind.

My adolescent daughters who are in the flower of youth never get sick.

The daughters are now so arrogant and rude that they don't even respond

to father's greetings.

Dad is devoting for self-cultivation by having hangover several times a

week!

군집

모든 동물은 무리지어 산다
개미도 사자도 고래도 멸치도… 자기들끼리 모여 산다

모여 사는 이유는 뭘까?

언어가 통해서
협동 사냥이 가능해서
안전을 위해서
생식을 위해서

사람들도 당연히 무리 지어 산다
아파트에 모여 살고 동네에 모여 살며 큰 도시도 만든다

휴일 아침인데 커피숍에 모여 수다 떠는
배불뚝이 아저씨들은 찐동물들이다

Flock together in groups

All animals live in groups

Ants, lions, whales, anchovies··· they all live together among themselves.

Why do we live together?

for language communicates with each other

for Cooperative hunting

for safety

for reproduction

Of course people live in groups too.

We live together in apartments, in neighborhoods, and form a big city.

The jelly-belly men who gather at coffee shops on holiday mornings to chat are Real animals.

관상의 실종 시대

창밖으로 지나는 사람들
골똘한 생각과 무언가의 고집으로 돌멩이 같은 얼굴을 하고 있다
헤헤거리고 펴진 얼굴은 아이들뿐
사는 것은 얼굴을 굳게 만드는 일인가
관상쟁이들이 할 일 없는 시대
내 얼굴도 굳어 있다

Times in which physiognomy disappeared

People passing by outside the window
because of their deep thoughts and stubbornness, they have a face like a
stone.
The only ones with bright smiles and open faces are children
Does living mean hardening your face?
The times when physiognomist have nothing to do
Also, my face becomes stiff

로맨스의 이유

도피처를 찾아 방황하는 사람들

안식처까지는 바라지도 않고
그저 쏟아지는 총탄을 피해
생존하고자 찾는 참호

그 참호에 독사가 있고
불발탄이 있어도
지금 당장 살아남아야 하기에

The reasons for Romance

People who are wandering in search of refuge

They don't even want a shelter
just avoid the rain of bullets
a trench in search of survival

Even if there's a poisonous snake in the trench,
unexploded bombs
but, right now they need to survive

또 주말

다시 홀로 마주한 나
열병처럼 사람 사이에서 휩쓸리고
기억도 안 나는 말들을 쏟아내며 보낸 시간

간은 살려달라 시들고
사지는 노곤하여 겨우 붙어있다

휴일 오전
쌩쌩한 사람들이 얼마나 있을까

다들 명 깎으며 바둥바둥하는 生들

Weekend comes again

I face myself again

swept among people like a fever

I spent pouring out words but even I don't remember

The liver is protesting, asking me to stop drinking

my limbs are exhausted and tired barely holding together

How many people are so energetic on a holiday morning

They are all struggling with their lives, sacrificing their own lives.

숫자

사람은 나고 자라면서 말을 배우듯 숫자를 배운다
하나 둘 셋

숨바꼭질 술래가 열을 세고
구슬치기하면서 숫자를 센다

나이가 들어가면서 성적도 인사고과도 업무성과도 숫자로 표시되고
계산기를 두들기며 돈을 센다

숫자 속에는 오로지 승과 패만 있다
사람은 사라지고 숫자만 남는다

Numbers

People learn numbers as they learn words as they grow up,

1, 2, 3

When playing Hide and Seek, the tagger counts to 10
and when Playing Marbles, we count number.

As we get older
work, performance evaluations, and work achievements are all expressed
in numbers
Also we count money by tapping on the calculator.

There are only wins and losses in numbers.
People disappear and only numbers remain.

내면 사냥

불편한 느낌
무엇인가
마음속을 들여다보니
그래, 그거였구나
살살 먹물을 뿜어대는 문어 한 마리
잡았다 이놈
이놈을 어찌할까나

Inner hunt

A feeling uncomfortable

I looked into my heart to see what it was

Yeah, that's it

There is an Octopus trying to squirt ink slowly

I got ya!

What should I do with this

기도

조그만 방에 들어앉아 세상을 봅니다
주변을 가늠하며, 거슬림이 없게 다듬고 채워보고요
부족하지도 과하지도 않게 그러나 편안할 수 있도록 배려하고 챙깁니다
그대들의 평안을 원합니다
나의 평안입니다

Pray

I sit in a small room and see the world

Assessing the surroundings,

I refine and fill them in so that they are not intrusive

Neither insufficient nor excessive

However, I consider and take care to ensure that you are comfortable

I want peace of all of you

It's my peace

아재의 슬픔

몸이 이젠 말을 듣지 않는다
시키지도 않았고 싫다는데도
혈당이 오르고 혈압도 지 멋대로다

힘내야 하는 순간에도 비실비실

난 인생을 착하고 순하게 살았는데
이 몸뚱어리가 왜 그런다니

좀 시키는 대로
착해질 수는 없는 거니?

Old man's sorrow

The physical condition is different from before

Even though I didn't order and

I said I didn't want to

but my blood sugar level goes up and blood pressure goes out of its own

way

Even when I need to be strong, I stagger

I've lived my life kind and gentle, but why is my body like this?

Can't I just be as good as I want ?

고급차

고급차가 지나간다
육중하게 살포시
미끄러지듯이 지나간다

나도 타고 잡다
고급차

Luxury car

A luxury car passes by
massive and gently
It passes like skidding

I want to have, too
the luxury car

심감대

성감대가 무뎌지는 나이가 되면
심감대가 발달한다.

눈물이 많아지고
가족들 사이에 있어도
외로움을 느끼는 나이라서 그런지

위로받으려 하고
기댈 사람이 필요해져서인지

손을 꼬옥 잡아주고
어깨를 감싸주는 접촉이
마음을 움직이게 한다

A mind sensing zone

When people reach an age where their erogenous zones become dull
the mind sensing zone develops.

Maybe it's because they have more tears than before
or reach an age where they feel lonely even among their family

or is it because they need comfort and someone to lean on

just the touch of holding hands and wrapping shoulder moves their heart.

사진

사진이 이런 거였나
사람을 놀래키는 기술이었네
거울 보면서도 몰랐네
이렇게 늙은 줄을

Photo

Was the photo like this?
it was a technique that shocked people
When I looked in the mirror but I didn't realize,
I was so old.

소유

땅 위에 금 긋고
바다를 선 그어
"내 꺼"라고 한 지가 얼마나 됐을까

나무와 동물들, 곤충들도 살아가는 지구에서
사람은 뭇 생명의 동의도 없이 "내 꺼"를 외친다

Possession

We set a limit on the ground
and draw a line in the sea
how long has it been since we said, "it's mine"?

On Earth where trees, animals, and insects live together
people claim "that's all mine!" without the consent of other living things.

멋진 여자

부드럽되 자존을 지키고
균형감각을 잃지 않아 대화가 즐거우며
주변을 거둬 먹이는 오지랖에
생명을 사랑하고
늙은 부모를 연민으로 돌보며
낭비하지 않고 아낀 돈으로 기부하는 생활이 몸에 배었고
경청하고 고개를 끄덕일 줄 아는데…

돈까지 버는 여자

A gorgeous woman

A woman who has a submissive personality but protects her self-respect,
pleasant to talk because she doesn't lose her balance of conversation,
cares for those around her, loves life,
and takes care of elderly parents with compassion,
is accustomed to donating money,
doesn't waste it and has a sound economic sense
even knows how to listen well
and is able to nod of sympathy.

Plus, a woman who earn good money

배롱나무꽃

사람 잡는 더위에 숨어 지내듯 하다가
눈가리개 한 경주마처럼 밥벌이를 하다가

숨 좀 쉬어져 옆을 보니 배롱나무꽃이 열대꽃처럼 생경하게 피었다

저 나무에 핀 진홍꽃은 어렴풋 작년에도 보았는데
여전히 낯설구나

정신없이 살다가 정신 차려 보는 꽃
배롱나무꽃

Flower of Lagerstroemia(The crimson flower)

It seemed like I was hiding from the sweltering
like a blindfolded racehorse, just trying to make a livelihood

after living like that
when I caught my breath a little, I looked to the side and saw a flowers of
Lagerstroemia are blooming unfamiliar, like a tropical flower

I vaguely remember the Crimson flowers blooming on that tree last year
too.
but it's still unfamiliar

The flower I saw when I came to my senses after living a life just looking
straight ahead
That's flower of Lagerstroemia

기다림

동물들의 징표가 기다림 아닐까

먹잇감을 노리는 치타도, 낚시하는 사람도 챌 때를 기다리고

비를 해를 달을 그녀를 그 남자를 엄마를 아빠를 자식손주를 월급을 손님을
졸업과 제대를 성년을 은퇴를 죽음을 기다리며

죽을 때까지 무언가를 기다리며 살아갑니다.

Waiting

Isn't the sign of living things just waiting?

We are waiting for the moment to catch
while a cheetahs are hunting
and people are fishing

We are waiting the rain, the sun, the moon, the man, the woman, the
mother, the father, the children, the grandchildren, the salary, the guests.

and graduation, getting discharged from the army, hitting legal age,
retirement and even death

So we live waiting for something until we die.

살아있는 이유

허약한 사람
양주 두 모금에 다리가 풀리고
세 모금에 땀이 나면서 정신도 몽롱한데
이 몸으로 어찌 버텨왔니
이 몸으로 어찌 살아갈거냐
그래도 내일 눈은 뜨겠지
아이들 학교 델다줘야지

Reason to be alive

A delicate person
just 2 sips of whisky make my legs loosened up
3 sips, I start to sweat and feel dizzy
How did I endure with a body like this?
How will I live with this physical condition from now on?
But when tomorrow morning comes, I will wake up
because I have to drop my children off at school

즐거울 수 있다면

모진 밥벌이에도
권력가들의 등쌀에도
저렴한 사회의식이 나라를 뒤덮고 있더라도
편을 가르고 공멸의 전투의식을 고취시키는
추한 입들이 득세하더라도

일하고 노래하고 책을 읽고 소주를 나누며
가족과 함께 너와 내가 즐거울 수 있다면

먹구름이 비가 되어 내리더라도
결국은 맑은 하늘이 예정되어 있음을 안다

If only we could be pleased

Even if it's a rough life to make a livelihood,

the annoying from the people in power,

the low social consciousness is sweeping the nation,

the disgusting mouths that divide sides or promote the battle spirit of co-destruction are becoming influential,

If only we can work, sing, read books and drink Soju together

If only you and I could be pleased with our families

The dark clouds turn into rain, though

I expect that clear skies are planned in the end

사장의 출퇴근

살금살금 걸어서
직원들 안 보는 사이 사무실로 들어간다

직원들이 귀신같이 알고
결재서류를 들고 노크한다
어찌 알았을까

퇴근할 때도 살금살금 사무실을 빠져나오는데
직원들이 이미 다 알고 있겠지
자유인이 됐음을

사장이 살금살금 출퇴근하는 이유가
지각과 조기 퇴근이 민망해서인데 직원들은 아려나

CEO's commute

Walks quietly and enters office when the employees don't look at me

But, the employees know like a demon that I'm here

and they knock with approval documents.

How did they know?

Even when the CEO leaves work, he sneaks out of the office.

But the employees must have known that they were freedom.

The reason the boss sneaks in and out of work is because he is embarrassed

about being late and leaving work early.

Do the employees realize this reason, really?

코로나

코로나에 걸렸네
요리조리 잘도 피해 다녔는데
까불까불 잘도 놀았었는데
코로나 창궐 3년도 더 지나 드디어 걸렸네
나도 이제 역사의 산증인
이제 앓기 시작했으니 살아남아야 산증인

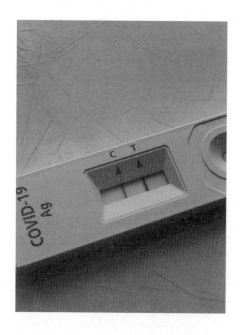

COVID-19

I got Covid

I avoided viruses here and there

I was wandering around

More than 3 years after the Pandemic broke out, I finally caught it

So now, I'm a living witness of history

But I'm starting to get sick from now, I have to survive to be living proof.

무제 2

초생달이 심하게 이뻐서
세상 시름 잊게 하니
오늘밤 소주는 건너뛰어도 되겠어

Untitled 2

Because the shape of crescent moon is so pretty

it made me forget all the worries of the world

So I think that I can skip drinking Soju tonight.

껍데기

우리는 얼마나 실체에 접근하고 살까
한쪽의 시선으로만 보고
한쪽의 각색된 이야기만 익숙하다
해석도 내가 원하는 방향으로 한다
자기 자신도 속이며 사는 마당에 남의 일, 세상일이야 오죽하겠나
껍데기라도 진짜 껍데기를 보면 다행이지

The shell(Appearance)

How approach do we live to reality?

We usually tend to see things from only one side and are familiar with only

one side's dramatized stories.

We tend to interpret in the direction we want to hear.

In a world where we live by deceiving ourselves,

how can we be so concerned about other people's affairs and many other

things?

Even if you look at the shell, it's a relief to see the real shell.

뻐꾸기와 매미

그대 주변을 맴돕니다
시답잖은 말을 건넵니다
눈길과 발길이 자꾸만 그대에게 향합니다
뒷산에서 뻐꾸기가 날아오릅니다
창밖 나무에선 매미가 맴맴 웁니다

Cuckoo and Cicada

I circles around you

I try to say something even nonsense

My eyes and steps keep turning towards you.

A cuckoo flies from the mountain behind

Cicadas are chirp-chirp crying in the trees outside the window.

인생

병고에 시달리다 보니
삶은 정지되고, 몸은 세월보다 더 쇠었다
무용한 것들이 아름다워지는 이유가
인간의 삶도 무용한 축에 낌을 알게 되어서인가
밤하늘 별을 보며
억겁의 시간과 무량한 공간을 마음으로만 담는다

Life

As I suffered acutely from illness,

life has come to a standstill, and the body has become weaker than time
has passed.

The reason why useless things feel beautiful

Is it because I learned that human life is also on the useless side?

Looking at the stars in the night sky, I capture eons of time and infinite
space in my heart.

빨간 날

휴일인 빨간 날
나도 쉬리라
사장이라고 못 쉬라는 법 있나
세상도 멈춘 날
빨간 날

A red letters day

On the red letters day of the holiday,
I will also take a day off
Is there a law that says, I can't rest just because I'm the boss
The day when the world stops
It's a red letters day

한 끗 차이

세상만사는 한 끗 차이로 갈린다
따진다고 따져봐도 거기서 거기 같은 한 끗
민중은 살아내느라 바빠 그 한 끗까지 신경 쓰지 못하고
머리만 좋은 나쁜 인간들은 그 한 끗을 챙겨 민중을 부린다

A slight difference

Everything in the world is divided by a slight difference.
Even if you think about it
it's just six of one and half a dozen
The public are too busy surviving to care about even a single detail,
but the bad people who are in power and only smart to care about that
single detail exploit the public

사유

저렇게 생각에 잠긴 동물을 본 적이 있는가?

동물도 가만히 있으면 무언가를 생각하는 것 같다고?

하지만 저렇게 반가부좌로 다리를 꼬고 앞다리를 얼굴에 괸 동물은 못 봤지?

Pensiveness

Have you ever seen a creature immersed in thought

Even animals seem to be thinking about something when they are still?

But have you never seen an animal like that with its legs crossed in a half-lotus position and its front legs resting on its face?

커피 친구 소주

아침 노곤함이 부르던 쓴 커피가 오후에 땡긴다
쓰다…
카페인이 또 잠 못 들게 하겠지

별 수 없다. 저녁에 소주로 잠을 불러야지

Soju, coffee's friend

The bitter coffee that

morning fatigue calls make me crave in the afternoon

It's bitter…

The caffeine will keep me from falling asleep again

There's nothing I can do, so I'll have to drink Soju to help me sleep in the

evening.

웃기는 세상

웃는다
재밌어 웃고
허해서 웃고
기가 차서 웃고
그지 같아서 웃고
슬퍼서 웃는다
그냥도 웃는다

The world makes me laugh

I laugh
I laugh for it's fun
I laugh for I feel empty
I laugh for I'm speechless
I laugh for even it's a crap situation
I laugh for even I'm sad
And I just laugh

현자

시간이 지나며
먼지도 흙도 나무의 나이테도 켜켜이 쌓이고
사람의 얼굴 주름도 층지는데

세월만큼 지혜로워진 현자는
토굴에 숨었는지 보이지 않고

늙어서 애가 된 사람들만
세상을 점령하고 있다

A wise man

As time goes by
dust, dirt, and tree growth rings pile up in several layers
and human facial wrinkles also form in layers

However, we cannot see a wise man who has become wiser over time they
are like hiding in a cave

Only 'big babies(old but immature people)' are taking over the world

위안

마음이 너무 허하고 외로워서
지구를 안고 잡니다

엎드려 가슴과 배를 바닥에 밀착시키면
지구가 위안을 줍니다

3층 방바닥이지만 땅과 연결되어 있으니
지구를 안은 것입니다

지구의 모든 산과 강과 바다와 생명을 안고
잠에 듭니다
나도 지구와 하나입니다

Comfort

I feel so empty and lonely that I sleep hugging the earth.

When I lie down and bring closer my chest and stomach to the floor,
the earth gives me comfort.

Even though it's on the 3rd floor, but it's connected to the ground
so it's about hugging the earth

I fall asleep
hugging all the mountains, rivers, seas, and life on the earth
I become one with the earth, too

지옥에서 살기

생로병사가 바탕인 사람의 생은
밥벌이까지 더하여 자체로 지옥이다

깨달음을 얻은 선각자는
지옥을 그나마 가볍게
때로는 행복할 수 있는 방법을 알려주었다

사랑
평화
우정
자연
자족
방아착
꿈
급기야는 아무 생각 말라는 무념무상까지

Living in hell

The life of a person whose life is based on birth, getting old, illness, dying the life, including making a livelihood, is hell in itself.

A pioneer who found enlightenment taught me
how to take hell a little lightly
or sometimes how to be able to be happy about accepting hell

Love

Peace

Friendship

Nature

Self-satisfaction

Releasing the attachments

Dream

In the end, even the point of being free from all thoughts, telling you not to think about any obsession

살과 뼈

아이가 살이 붙고 키가 자라
마침내 성인이 되는 과정은 사랑이다

부모가 돌보든, 젖동냥으로 크든, 늑대가 키우든
스스로 기적처럼 벌레를 잡아먹고 크든

사람의 살과 뼈는
뭇 생명과 대자연이 키운 사랑의 결정체다

Flesh and bones

The kids gained weight and grow taller
finally, the process of becoming an adult is love.

Whether kids are cared for by their parents, raised through begging breast
milk, or raised by wolves
or raised by miraculously catching and eating insects on their own

Human flesh and bones are
the fruits of love fostered by all living things and Mother Nature.

고래의 꿈

육지에서 걷던 고래가 정말 날고 싶어서 바다로 간 걸까
바닷속에서는 새처럼 날 수 있다지
두려웠을 검은 바다를 헤치고 나아가
고래는 고래 적에 꿈을 이루었구나
그래서 고랜가?

Whale's dream

Did the whale that was walking on land really want to fly so it went to the
sea
People say whales can fly like birds in the sea
The whale must have achieved a dream in old days moving through the
fearful black sea
So the name of whale means old days?
(korean 'gorae' has two means, whale and old days)

결혼의 이유

나이가 더 들기 전에 그냥 하고
상대의 직업이 괜찮아서 하고
살림할 사람이 필요해서 하고
아이 낳기 힘들기 전에 얼른 하고
혼자 살기 적적해서 하고
부모님 성화에 못 이겨서 하고

어쩌다 사랑에 겨워서 하고

Reasons for marriage

People just get married before getting older,
for a partner had a better job,
for need someone to take care of the house.
People get married earlier before it becomes difficult to have children,
for living alone feel them lonely.
People get married because they couldn't overcome the parents' nagging

And people get married for happening to fall in love.

낙천주의자를 꿈꾸며

다 잘될 거야
나는 그냥 웃을 일만 있어
힘든 거? 없어
그냥 좋게 생각하면 돼
세상은 즐겁기만 해
비가 와도 좋고
해가 떠도 좋고
지진이 와도 좋고
전쟁 나도 좋아
염세주의는 안 돼
이러다 정신병원에 갇혀도 좋아야 돼

Dreaming of being an Optimist

Everything will be alright

There will only be things to smile about for me

Am I having a hard time these days? Nope!

Just think positively

The world is just fun for us

It's okay even if it rains

It's okay if the sun rises

It's okay if there's an earthquake

It's okay if war breaks out.

No Pessimism!

Even if I stay like this and end up in a psychiatric hospital,

but have to be okay.

시들시들

시들어가는 친구와
시들어가는 내가 오랜만에 소주를 마셨다

거나하면 숨어있던 호기가 살아나
노래하고 부비적대던 우리가
이젠 조용히 집으로 간다

익어가는 거라고 하고 싶지만
머리털이 빠지고 있으므로
명백하게 시들어가는 것이 맞다

Wither wither

A withering friend and I drank Soju been a while since we drank together

We used to sing and dance freakly as if our hidden brave spirit came alive
when we had a drink before
but now, both of us just have a drink and then quietly go home.

We wanted to think that we are ripening but
because our hair is falling out
it's true that we are clearly withering away.

나이 대별 윗대에 대한 감흥

10대 때는 20대가 나이 든 성인들이고

20대 때는 30대가 시들어가는 사람들 같고

30대 때는 40대가 중년으로 보이고

40대 때는 50대가 노인의 시작처럼 보이고

50대 때는 60대가 이젠 노인이라 짠해 보인다

60대 때는 70대가 곧 세상을 하직할 나이로 보이고

70대 때는 80대가 용케 살아남은 거북이처럼 보이고

80대 때는 90대가 명줄 긴 송장처럼 보이고

90대 때는 주위에 같은 90대도 찾기 힘들다

그리고 모든 세대를 살아온 나는 항상 젊었다

Inspiration for older people in each age group

Teenagers think about that people in their 20s are like mature adults

In your 20s, they think about that people in their 30s are withering away

In your 30s, they think about that people in their 40s look like middle-aged.

In your 40s, they think about that people in their 50s seem like the beginning of the eldrly

In your 50s, they think about that people in their 60s are really old people so they feel sad and a little bit bitter.

In your 60s, they think about that people in their 70s are the age to leave this world.

In your 70s, they think about that people in their 80s look like Turtles which somehow managed to survive.

In your 80s, they think about that people in their 90s look like a Corpse with a long lifeline.

In your 90s, it's hard to even find people in their 90s like friends.

And I, who through all those generations have always been young.

짤 중독

읽던 책 두 장 넘기고 뭔가를 하려고 집어든 핸드폰

뭘 하려고 했는지는 까맣게 잊고
왜 짤을 보고 있는지도 모르고
혼자 히히덕거리고 있다

Addiction of short-form contents

Only turned 2 pages of the book I was reading and picked up my cell phone to do something

I completely forgot what I was going to do
without even knowing why I'm looking at the short-form
I'm just burst out laughing alone

양말의 비밀

신발 속 양말 신은 발이 미끄러지지 않고
걷는데도 추진력이 있다
약간 습기가 있는 맨발 느낌의
신발 속 접지가 환상적이다.
신발을 벗어보니
양말 바닥 한가운데
걷기 편한 추진력과 접지력의 비밀이
빼꼼 안녕 한다.

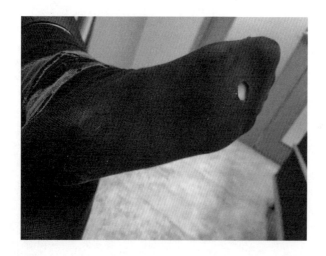

The secret of socks

Feet wearing socks inside shoes don't slip

and there is propulsion in walking

The ground connection in the shoes is fantastic as it feels like bare feet with

a little humidity.

When I took off my shoes, the secret -propulsion and ground connection

that make walking comfortable- was revealed in the middle of the bottom

the sock

에너지 이론

비에 흠뻑 젖은 나무는
숲의 모든 나무들과 함께
시냇물을 만들어 가재와 송사리를 키운다.

햇볕 따뜻한 논에는
노란 벼 아래
미꾸라지와 우렁이 가족도 산다.

달이 뜨고 지고,
차고 기우는 갯벌에서는
망둑어와 농발게도 제 삶을 산다

자연은
에너지를 보존하지 않고 무한 확대한다.

Energy theory

A tree soaked in rain joins force together with all the trees in the forest to create a stream, which grows crayfish and minnow.

In the warm and sunny rice fields, families of loaches and pond snails live under the yellow rice paddy

In the mudflats where the moon rises and sets, waxes and wanes, gobiid fish and fiddle crabs live their own lives.

Nature doesn't conserve energy but expands it infinitely.

시간의 힘

어르신들은
세월이라고 하였다

시간을 기다리지 못하는 성질 급한 사람과
시간을 감당하지 못할 만큼 크나큰 아픔 속에서 길을 잃은 사람의 귀에는
들리지 않겠지만

시간은 분명
세상의 모든 것들을
지금도 똑딱똑딱 바꾸고 있다

그래서 어르신들은 세월이라고 하였다

Power of time

The elders were called time and tide

With an impatient person who can't wait for time
It may not be heard by the ears of someone
who is lost in a pain so heavy that time cannot bear it

But time is definitely changing everything in the world, by tick-tock

That is why the elders were called time and tide

똑딱똑딱

똑딱똑딱 시계 소리
시곗바늘 가는 소리

세상만사 변화 소리
똑딱똑딱 세월 소리

Tick tock

Tick tock is sound of clock
The sound of clock's hands ticking

The sound of changing everything in the world
Tick tock is the sound of time and tide

사랑

가만히 살펴보면 나는 사랑을 믿지 않는다
상처가 무서워서가 아니고
나 자신을 믿지 않아서 그렇다
내가 나를 바닥까지 사랑했던가
스스로에 대한 채찍질과
몰아붙이던 지난 삶을 돌이켜보면
나는 나 자신조차 사랑해본 적이 없어 보인다
그래서 나는 너의 사랑도 믿지 못하고
나의 너에 대한 사랑도 불안하다

The love

When I look at me quietly, I don't believe in love
Not because I'm afraid of getting hurt
but because I don't believe in myself.
Did I love even the worst version of myself?
When I look back on my past life of whipping and pushing myself,
it seems like I've never even loved myself.
So I can't even believe in your love
and my love for you is also insecure

가장들

섭이 아부지가
직장 근처 밥집에서
혼자 김치찌개에
소주를 먹고 집에 간다

훈이 아부지도
혼자 빈 사무실에 앉아
땅콩에 소주를 먹고 집에 간다

용이 아부지와 삼이 아부지는
용케 광명 읍네서 만나 밥집에서
소주를 나눈다

금요일 밤은
술을 먹어야
집에 갈 수 있나 보다

Breadwinners

Seop's father

has a Kimchi stew(Kimchi-jjigae) and drinks Soju alone

at a bistro near workplace

and then goes home

Hoon's father

sits alone in the empty office,

drinks Soju with peanuts

and then goes home, too

Yong's father and Sam-i's father

meet by coincidence at Gwang-myeong town and they drink Soju together

at a bistro

Perhaps the breadwinners need to drink alcohol for being able to go home

on Friday night.

예의 바른 일본 사람들

스미마셍 아리가또
일본 거리에서 차 소리만큼 계속 들리는 소리

예의 바르고 겸손한 표현이 생활화된 교양 있어 보이는 모습들

한 치의 실수도
용납되지 않는 무서운 사회
적국의 포로가 돼도
미안하다고 고개 숙이는 사람들

칼 찬 사무라이들이
무서운 세상에서 살아남기 위해 체화된
예의 바름 속에 숨겨진 굴종

The Japanese people who are polite

すみません (I'm sorry), ありがとう (Thank you)

These two are heard as constantly as the sound of cars on the Japanese streets

Expressions of politeness and humility has become part of daily life in Japan appearances of cultured Japanese people

A scary society where not even a single mistake is tolerated,
people who bow their heads in apology even if they become prisoners of war from the enemy country

The submission that Samurai with swords at their waists hide in the embodied politeness in order to survive in a scary Japanese society

관계

예의와 매너가 필요한 관계
한 치의 방심도 허용되지 않는
5성급 호텔 서비스 같은 관계

욕도 하고 장난도 치고
울어도 가만히 바라봐 주며
술 먹고 토해도 창피하지 않은
동네 여인숙 같은 관계

그래선지 5성급 호텔은 불편하다

Relationship

A relationship that requires courtesy and manners
A relationship like the service of a 5-star hotel, where no one is allowed to
let off guard

A relationship like that of a local inn where I can curse, play a joke on,
but they just look on even when I cry,
and not be ashamed even if I drink and throw up

Maybe that's why 5-star hotels are uncomfortable.

토끼

먹이사슬 아랫동네 사는 토끼는
항상 슬펐다

늘 경계하고 두려워하며
도망쳐야 하는 토끼라서
자기를 보고 도망치는 개구리가 좋았다

개구리야 같이 놀자 쫓아가도
개구리는 무서워 더 도망을 갔다

불쌍한 토끼는 또 슬펐다

Rabbit

The rabbit living at the bottom of the food chain was always sad

The rabbit, who was always on guard, afraid
and had to run away
so the rabbit liked the frog because it's afraid of the rabbit

Even though the rabbit said, "Let's play together" and looked for the frog,
the frog got even more scared and ran away.

The poor rabbit was sad again

편의점

24시간 영업규칙상
어거지로 문 연다는 볼멘 편의점

밤 늦어 인적 없는
동네골목에 홀로 불 밝힌 등대 같은 편의점

귀갓길에 등도 시리고
마음도 시려서
괜시리 들어가보는 편의점

Convenience store

A grouchy convenience store that is forced to open under the rule of being open 24 hours a day

A convenience store like a lighthouse that lights up alone late at night on deserted town's alley

A convenience store that I decided to go into because my back and heart was cold on the way home

출근의 의미

아침 눈뜨면 어딘가 갈 곳이 있다

그곳에 가면 사람들이 있고
소소한 수다도 떨 수 있다

주어진 역할로
머리도 아프지만
그 역할이 또 나를 증명한다

다시 내일을 기약하며
소주잔을 나누고
통닭이라도 사들고 귀가하는
의기양양한 발걸음

출근은 인생에 엄청난 의미가 있다

The meaning of going to work

When I open my eyes in the morning, there is somewhere to go

When I go there, there are people
I can chatter, too

A role that given to me makes me get annoyed but that role proves me
again

The triumphant step way back home with a promise of tomorrow, sharing
Soju, and then carrying at least a fried chicken

Going to work has tremendous meaning in life.

헛바늘

며칠 술에 헛바늘이 섰다

바늘로 찌르듯 하는 걸 보니
방탕했던 몸을 벌주는가 보다

오늘도 술빽이 친구가 살살 꼬시고는 있지만
알딸딸 술 재미가 생각나지 않는다

The sore on my tongue

Drinking for several days in a row, I have sore on the tongue

I feel as if it's being pricked by a needle so it seems like punishing my body
that has been debauched

Even today, my friend who is a heavy drinker are lightly asking with me
but there is no fun in buzzed drinking

어느 가을날

햇빛 눈부신 가을 낮

오늘은 꽃이 필 것 같고
개구리도 뛰놀 것처럼 화창하다

시들어감을 거부하는 아지매의 화장 같은 날

만춘 같은 만추에 나도 일찍 집에 가보련다

One autumn day

A dazzling autumn day with sunlight

It's beautiful today that it looks like flowers will bloom and frogs will play around too.

A day like the make-up of an old lady who refuses to wither away

Due to late autumn like the end of spring, I'm planning to go home early today

상실의 시대

먹고살 만하고
전쟁도 없다
병원도 골라 간다

아버지는 조금 먼저 가셨지만 어머니도 계시고
형제자매들도 무탈한 편이다
속 썩이는 자식들이야 철들면 낫겠지

상실을 상실한 시대
나름 태평하지 아니한가

The era of loss

Just enough to make a living

there is no war

we can also choose the hospital we want to go

My father passed away a little earlier but mother is still alive

and my siblings tend to be safe and sound

even if there are children who act up, they will get better when they

become mature

The era that loses loss

Isn't it somewhat carefree?

밤 산책

시장에 갑니다
오늘은 열심히 사는 사람들을 보려고 가는 것이 아닙니다
시장 한쪽 구석에 분명 국화꽃이 무데기로 있을 듯해서 보러 가네요
지난번 산책 때는 초록 꽃대에 꽃망울이 조금 비쳤거든요
머 호떡도 조금 땡기네요

Night walking

I'm going to the market.

Today, it's not for seeing people who are living hard in market.

There seems to be a bunch of chrysanthemums in a corner of the market, so I go to look at them.

Last time when I went for a walk, there were some flower buds on the green stalks

Well, I have a bit of an appetite for Hotteok(Griddlecake with sugar filling) too.

만추

낙엽처럼 껍질만 남아
고독한 냄새는 갈색으로 풍기고

아릿하게 허한 가슴은 허허벌판을 헤매는 듯하다

이 쥐일 놈의 만추는 늙어가는 나와 왜 이리 닮은 것이냐

Late autumn

Only the bark remains like fallen leaves
the brown smell of solitude wafts out

And my heart which feels something missing, a little sore
feels like wandering in an empty plain.

Why does this late autumn like enemy bear so much resemblance to me as
I grow older?

칠십억 길

칠십억 명 우리들이 헤쳐 나가는 칠십억 인생길
개미들아 너희들은 칠천억 마리? 칠천억 개미생길이니?
인식하는 세상은 개미 똥꼬멍만큼 작지만
개미야 사람아 우리는 아무도 알 수 없는 길을 홀로 걸어가는 나그네들
우리 길 가다 만나거든 악수는 못 할망정 밟지는 말자꾸나

7 billion ways

The 7 billion ways of life that 7 billion people get through

Hey ants! Are you 700 billion ants? so, is there a 700 billion ant's life way?

The world we perceive is as small as an ant's butthole

however, ants! people! we are travelers walking alone on a way that no

one knows

If we meet each other on the way, we may not shake hands but let's not

step on.

천천히

흘러내리는 용암이 식어 들판이 될 만큼이나 천천히 천천히
바위가 모래로 될 만큼이나 천천히 천천히
뽕밭이 바다로 변할 만큼 천천히 천천히
바닷속 산이 우뚝 솟아 나무가 자라는 산이 될 만큼이나 천천히 천천히
은하수 별이 사람으로 날 만큼이나 천천히 천천히

세상은 천천히 천천히 서로가 하나임을 보여 줍니다

Slowly

Slowly slowly,

as much as the flowing lava so slowly cools that becomes a field

Slowly slowly,

as much as the rocks turn into sand

Slowly slowly,

as much as the mulberry field turns into the sea

Slowly slowly,

as much as the mountain in the sea rises so high that it becomes a mountain

where trees grow

Slowly slowly,

as much as the stars in the Milky Way galaxy are born as humans

Slowly slowly,

the world shows us we are the one.

삶

- -

슬픔과 고통은 당연한 거라 새삼스러울 거 없다
딛고 서있는 땅처럼 여기자

그리고 그 위에서 즐거움과 사랑과 낭만과 감성을 깨워 보자
웃으며 때로는 울면서 얼싸안고 살아보자

Life

- -

Sadness and pain are natural
so it's nothing new
Let's treat it like the ground we stand on

And let's awaken joy, love, romance, and emotion on it
Let's live our lives embracing each other, laughing and sometimes crying

기다림의 색

기다림에는
조바심이 스며들기도
설레임이 스며들기도
두려움이 스며들기도
행복감이 스며들기도
괴로움이 스며들기도
간절함이 스며들기도
하여서 그 색깔은 제각각 다릅니다

The colors of waiting

Sometimes impatience seeps into the waiting,

sometimes excitement seeps into,

sometimes fear seeps into,

sometimes happiness seeps into,

sometimes pain seeps into,

sometimes eagerness seeps into.

So the colors of the waiting are different respectively.

사람의 상처

닭은 알을 품고
개도 새끼를 품어 키우지

사람은 자식만 품지 않고
친구도 품고 여자도 품고 남자도 품지

동물은 새끼만 품고
사람은 다 큰 사람까지 품지

그래서 사람은 동물과 다른 상처가 생기지

People's wounds

Chicken incubates eggs

even dogs have puppies and raise them

People don't just embrace their children

but they embrace friends, women,

and men too.

Animals only embrace their cubs

but people embrace adults as well.

That's why people get different wounds than animals.

만남

사람의 만남은 영혼과 영혼의 만남

영혼에는 외모도 돈도 지위도 권세도 딸려오지 않아서
원래 만남은 반발하는 반응이 없는 것이다

마치 바람이 섞이듯
마치 안개가 섞이듯
영혼의 만남은 그러한 것이다

The meeting

The meeting of people is the meeting of soul and soul

Originally soul don't come with looks, money, status, or power
so there is no reaction against meeting each other.

As if the winds are mixing together
As if the fogs are mixing together,
that's what soul's meeting is like.

김치

헬조선이라고 공감합니다
자본주의 세상이 된 지금 경쟁 속에서 다들 힘듭니다

하지만 이 땅에는 김치가 있지요
사시사철 때마다 다양한 김치도 있고요
김장은 또 얼마나 지혜로운가요
그래서 이 땅을 못 떠나겠습니다

어떤 여행가가 세계를 떠돌다 아팠는데 한국 영사관에서 된장찌개와 김치를
먹고 씻은 듯이 나았다지요

식당도 김치 맛이 좋은 집을 찾아가는 사람인데 헬조선이라고 떠나겠나요

세계 어디서든 김치를 살 수 있다고요?
영사관 김치도 산 거였다고요?
하와이에는 김치공장도 있다고요?

이제 떠야 하나…

Kimchi

I agree with the word 'Hell-Joseon(Korea is like hell)'.

Now we have become a capitalist world, everyone is having a hard time in the overheated competition.

But there is Kimchi in this country.

There are various types of kimchi for each season.

How wise are the principles of Kimchi-making?

So I can't leave this country.

It's said that a traveler got sick while traveling around the world, but felt better after eating Doenjang-jjigae(soybean paste stew) and Kimchi given to him by the Korean consulate.

The people who prefer going restaurants with tasty Kimchi are Koreans, so do you think they will easily leave Korea because it's Hell-Joseon?

Everyone can buy Kimchi anywhere in the world?

Was the Kimchi from the consulate for sale?

Is there even a Kimchi factory in Hawaii?

Should I leave now⋯

부모와 자식

세상 부모들은 무조건 자식 편입니다
모든 것이 용서되지요

반대로 자식은 즈그들 편입니다
부모의 잘못을 용서하지 않아요

태생부터 부모에 의지해 살아서 생각의 시작점이 다른 이유인 것 같습니다

그나마 철이 들고 또 들어 부모를 지 자식마냥 안쓰럽게 바라볼 수 있어야 부
모의 삶을 이해하겠지요

부모는 조심히 살아야 합니다
자식이 철들기는 하늘의 별따기 마냥 어려워서입니다

세상 무서운 건 자식의 눈입니다

Parents and children

Parents around the world are always on their children's side.
Everything is forgiven

On the contrary, children are on their own side.
They don't forgive parents' mistakes.

I think that's why their starting points of thinking are different because they
have been dependent on their parents since birth.

Only when they become mature enough and can look at parents with pity
as if their own children
and then, they will be able to understand the lives of parents.

This is because children mature enough is as difficult as 'finding stars in the
sky(like getting blood from a stone = almost impossible)'

The scariest thing in the world is a child's eyes.

나

나를
나도
나의
나에게
나는
내가…

생각의 대부분을 차지하는 나 중심사고
결국 번뇌의 중심이 되고…

나를 잊으면, 버리면, 놓으면 죽음인가 해탈인가

죽거나 해탈해야 벗어나는 '나'라는 족쇄
잠이 좋다. 잠시 해탈하니…

I

Me

me, too

my

to me

I am

I···

Me-centered thinking that takes up most of my thoughts.

In the end, such ways of thinking become the center of agony···

If I forget myself,

if I abandon myself,

if I let go,

is it death or liberation?

The shackles of 'me' that can only be escaped if I die or become liberated.

I like sleep. It's only for a moment but I can be liberated···

땅 욕심

거의 핏빛에 가까운 황토밭을 보면
평평하게 골라진 예쁜 밭을 보면
소유욕구가 샘솟는다

시골에서 자랐지만 지금은 도시에서 자본주의의 첨병 같은 직업을 가졌음에
도 곡식이 잘 자라는 땅을 그냥 보지 않는다

세포 깊숙이 농자의 피가 흐른다고 느끼지만
더 깊숙이는 소유욕이 아니라 생존욕구이리라

지금은 돈에 비유될 수 있으려나
가족을 먹이는 방법은 기름진 땅을 갈고 곡식을 키우는 것이 거의 유일한
시절이 있었을 테니.

Greed for land(Desire of field)

When I look at the red clay field, which is almost the color of blood,
When I look at a pretty, flat field,
my desire of possess arises.

Even though I grew up in the countryside and now have a job at the forefront of capitalism in the city, I don't just look at the land where crops grow well.

I can feel the farmer's blood flowing deep in my cells,
but even deeper, it's not a desire to possess but a desire to survive.

Can it be compared to money now?
Perhaps there was a time when plowing fertile land and growing grains was almost the only way to feed family members

정답

학원도 학교도 답 고르기 훈련장입니다
종교도 자기들만이 답이라고 합니다
힘겨운 순례 길도 답을 위해서라면 마다하지 않습니다

사람들이 평생 답을 찾아다닙니다
혼자서 되는대로 정답이라고 정하기도 합니다

세상을 다 살기 전에 정답을 다 아는 사람으로 무장하려고 합니다
내가 정한 답과 다른 답에 대해서는 거부하고 이기려 합니다

사람이 어리석어 그럴까 심심해서 그럴까도 생각해 봅니다

사람들이 정답을 가지고 피 터지게 싸울 때도
세월은 아무 생각 없이 흐릅니다

예나 지금이나 자연은 그냥 피고 지고 또 피고 집니다

Right answer

The private educational institutes and schools are also training grounds for choosing the right answer.

Religions also say they're the only one answer.

They don't mind going on a pilgrimage for the right answer.

People spend their whole lives looking for the right answer

Sometimes they decide on their own it's the right answer.

Before going through all the world, they want to arm themselves with someone who knows all the right answers.

They reject, tries to win about answers that are different from the right answer they has chosen

I wonder if it's because people are stupid, or if it's because they're bored.

Even when people fight bloody battles over the right answer, time and tide passes by without any thoughts

Now and then, nature just blooms and falls, blooms and falls again.

시인의 침묵

시인이 절필을 하거나
시를 쓸 수 없는 처지라면
세상이 험해져서 그렇다

탄광의 카나리아처럼
감성의 촉수를 세상에 드리운 시인이 말문을 닫는다면
그건 분명 세상 탓이다

나쁜 놈들이 득세해서 착한 사람들이 힘들 것이고
힘든 사람들끼리 기대지도 못하게 분열시키고 있을 것이다

말문이 막힌 지 꽤 되었다는 좋아하는 시인의 독백이 가슴을 아프게 한다

A poet's silence

If a poet gives up writing or is unable to write poetry,
that's because the world has become rough

If a poet, who has spread his emotional tentacles to the world like a
Canary(kink of bird: Lark) in a coal mine keep silent
it's definitely the world's fault.

The bad guys will gain power and the good guys will have a hard time.
It will divide people who are having a hard time so they can't even depend
on each other.

The monologue of my favorite poet, who said it had been a while since he
was speechless, breaks my heart.

민족성

외세와 그에 굴종하는 자들이 한민족은 분열하는 기질을 가졌다며 욕합니다

조선시대 당파분쟁을 예로 들며 편을 나누어 싸운다고 민족성이 저열하답니다

자기들은 천황의 영도 아래 일사분란함의 획일성을 보이는 우수민족이라고 합니다

각자의 의견을 가지고 표현하며 이합집산하여 합의점을 찾아가는 모습은 현대의 바람직한 민주주의 상입니다
개인이 존중받는 세상입니다

아이러니합니다
한민족을 욕하던 그 외세와 배신자들이 떠받드는 나라는 민주주의 표본인 미국입니다
피부색과 인종과 지역과 출신국가가 다 달라 생각도 이념도 기질도 총천연색 용광로 같은 나라 미국을 숭배합니다

외세와 배신자들에 속지 맙시다
우리 민족은 서양의 르네상스와 민주주의 경험을 거치지 않고도 체화된 사람 중심 민주주의 민족입니다

Ethnicity

The Foreign Influence and those who submit to them criticize the Korean people for having a tendency to divide.

Factional Strife during the Joseon Dynasty as an example, people divide into sides and fight, showing that their ethnicity is inferior.

They say that they are an excellent people who show neatness and uniformity under the leadership of the Emperor.

Expressing one's own opinions and coming together to reach a consensus is a desirable image of modern democracy.
A world where individuals are respected

It's ironic
the country supported by foreign powers and traitors who cursed the Korean people is the United States, a model of democracy.

They worship America, a country like a melting pot of all colors, with different skin colors, races, regions, and countries of origin, and different thoughts, ideologies, and temperaments.

Let us not be deceived by foreign powers and traitors.
Our people are a people-centered democracy that was realized without going through the Western Renaissance and democratic experience.

역사의 진보

인간역사의 진보방식은 나선형이라는데 퇴행한 지금은 괴롭다

데자뷰처럼 나타나는 인간 말종들을 봐주기도 괴롭다

사람의 머리에서 가슴까지가 제일 멀다는데 국가와 사회는
오죽할까 싶으니 더 괴롭다

나선형으로나마 조금씩 나아가면 그나마 다행이고
과거로 회귀해서 돌아오지 못하는 나라도 여럿 있다 하니 두렵다

Progress of history

The progression of human history is said to be a spiral, but now that we have regressed, it is painful.

It's painful to look at the scums that appear like déjà vu.

It says the furthest distance is from a person's head to their heart.
I wonder how bad the country and society they are,
so I'm painful even more

At least it's good if we're moving forward little by little in a spiral
but I'm afraid there are many countries that have gone back to the past

겨울

겨울이 되면 아프기 시작했다
겨우내 봄을 기다리며 아팠다
낙엽수조차 아픈 나 같아 싫었다
열대지방을 고향인 양 그리워하는 겨울이었다

그 겨울이 이제 시작되려 한다

Winter

I started feeling sick in the winter

I was sick waiting for spring all winter

I hated even the deciduous tree because they seemed like me who was sick

It's a winter in which I longed for the tropics as if it were my home

The winter is about to begin

나의 해방일지

얽매이지 않은 삶이 어디 있나요
너도 나도 울 아부지도 얽매이고 삽니다
술로 풀고 때로는 밥상도 엎으며 삽니다

그런데 해방의 날은 언제 오나요
곧 옵니다
희망을 가지고 술도 푸고 밥상도 엎읍시다
까짓 거 오고야 말겠지요

My Liberation Notes

Where can there be a life that is not tied down with somewhere.
You and I, my father live like they are tied down with somewhere too
We vent our anger by drinking, sometimes by overturning the meal table

Then, when will the liberation day come?
It's coming soon
Let's drink and overturn the meal table with hope
That day will come anyway

연탄 봉사

도심 외곽에 비켜난 사람들
세월에 비켜난 연탄을 아직도 땐다

어르신들은 고마움에 괜스레 안절부절못하시고
뜻 맞아 모인 사람들은 왁자지껄 웃으며 줄지어 선다

몸은 삐그덕거리며 땀을 내고
얼굴은 어느새 검댕이 묻어가는데
마음은 아래로 아래로 낮아진다

The briquette delivery volunteer

People who moved aside from the outskirts of the city center
they still use coal briquettes that have moved aside by time

The elderly are so thankful that they can't help but feel restless
and like-minded people gather in a line, laughing loudly.

Their body creaks and sweats
and soot from the briquettes is covering their face, though
the heart goes lower and lower(becomes humble)

목장갑 짜는 기계

오래된 골목 허름한 구옥의 일층 상가에 쉬지 않고 돌아가는 목장갑 짜는 기계가 있습니다

출퇴근하며 걷다가 드르륵거리는 기계에 정신이 팔립니다
어떤 때는 그 기계를 보려고 부러 그 골목으로 지나갑니다

그 집의 주인이 누군지 궁금해졌습니다
기계 하인을 두고서는 밤낮으로 놀러 다니는지 한 번도 얼굴을 보지 못했거든요

나도 기계 하인이 나 대신 돈벌이를 하면 좋겠다는 꿈이 생겼더랬지요
술 마시고 걸을 때는 한참을 바라보다 갔답니다

벤쯔자동차보다 더 갖고 싶습니다
목장갑 짜는 기계 하인

A machine for weaving work gloves

On the 1st floor of a shabby old house in an old alley, there is a weaving work gloves machine operates non-stop.

While walking to and from work, I often get distracted by a rattling machine.

Sometimes I deliberately pass through that alley just to see the machine.

I wondered who the owner of that house was.
I guess the owner who has the mechanical servant and hangs around day and night, but I've never seen the owner's face.

I also had a dream of having a mechanical servant make money for me.
When I was drinking and walking, I looked at the machine for a while before leaving.

I'd rather have a mechanical servant that weaves work gloves than a Mercedes-Benz car.

날씨

식당에서 덥다며 에어컨을 켜달라는 손님

아침나절 훈풍이 불더니 소나기처럼 비가 내린다

평화로운 일상의 모습처럼 보이지만…

지금은 엄동설한이어야 마땅한 12월 중순 한반도

갑자기 재난영화의 도입부 장면으로 바뀌지 않았는가?

Weather

A customer who says that it's hot in a restaurant and asks to turn on the air conditioner.

Warm breeze blew in the midmorning, then rain fell like a shower.

It looks like a peaceful everyday life, but···

It's mid-December on the Korean Peninsula, which should be a harsh winter right now.

Didn't it suddenly turn into the introductory scene of the disaster movies?

도반

마음을 알고 비워내는 공부를 하며 함께하는 이들이 도반이 된다
산사에서 수련원에서 치열하게 마음공부를 하는 도반들

세상에 나온 순간부터 생멸과 삶의 의미를 고민하는 숙명을 진 인간종

길거리, 식당, 버스 안, 친구 모임, 학교, 직장… 거하는 곳이 산사이고 수련원
이며 만나는 누구나 도반이 된다

Do-ban(The companion who cultivate the moral sense together)

Those who study together to understand and empty the mind become Do-ban

companion who study their minds intensely at mountain temples and training centers

A human species destined to worry about life and death and the meaning of life from the moment they come into the world

On the street, in a restaurant, on a bus, at a friend's gathering, at school, at work··· where you live is the mountain temple and training center, and everyone you meet becomes your companion.

바깥양반의 송년

연말 술을 물보다 더 먹습니다
노곤해도 일상이 되었네요

우정도 존재감도 확인하는 송년 술자리
직장에서도 마무리 방점이 필요합니다

왁자지껄한 모임자리
소소한 마음을 나누며 한 해를 추억합니다

그리곤 케이크 하나 사들고 집으로 무사히 귀환해야
가족들의 눈총에도 무사할 수 있습니다

Year-end of my husband

At the end of the year, he drinks more alcohol than water.
Even though he's tired, it's become a daily routine.

A year-end drinking party that confirms friendship and existence.

Even at work, an emphasis on finishing is necessary.
A noisy gathering place,
he shares small thoughts and reminisces about the year.

Then he has to buy a cake and return home safely,
so he can be safe from the glares of his family.

개

요새 딸아이들의 언어에 개가 두루 쓰인다
개웃긴다, 개재밌다, 개많다, 개억울, 개이득…

고양이를 제치고 개가 선택된 이유는…
교감의 정도라기보다는…
듣는 개는 기분 나쁘겠지만…
개 같거나 개보다 못한 인간이 더 많아져서는 아닌지…
하여 거칠어진 세상을 살다 보니 말이 세진 건 아닌지…

나도 오늘은 개화나고 개슬프다

Emphasis prefix 'Ge'(which means 'so'/as same Korean pronounciation with 'Dog')

These days, 'Ge' is widely used in our daughters' language.

Ge hilarious = So hilarious, Ge fun = so fun, Ge many = so many, Ge unfair = so unfair, Ge beneficial = so beneficial···

The reason dogs were chosen over cats···

Rather than the degree of sympathy···

The dog that hears it may feel bad, but···

Like a dog or isn't it because there are more humans who are worse than dogs

or

as we live in a rough world, I wonder if they have become harsher in saying

I'm also 'Ge(so)' angry and 'Ge(so)' sad today.

노인의 식탁

식탁 위에 탈지우유 팩 몇 개가 쌓여있고
하얀 약봉지도 몇 개나 있네요
자그마한 꿀단지 위에 숟가락이 얹어져 있고 영수증들과 메모지가 뒹굽니다

노인은 내복에 겉옷까지 걸치고 앉아 안경 너머로 핸드폰이 바쁩니다
자식들과의 단체톡방 수다가 여전히 자식들과 함께하는 식탁인 양 외로움을
덜어줍니다

노인은 가끔 홀로 남은 인생과 지나온 삶이 서글프지만 그래도 살아갈 힘은
충분히 얻고 있습니다

Old man's table

There are several cartons of skim milk piled up on the table

There are also a few white medicine bags

A spoon is placed on top of a small jar of honey

Receipts and notes are lying around

The old man is sitting in his underwear and outerwear, busy looking at his cell phone through his glasses.

Chatting in a group KakaoTalk chat room with children alleviates the loneliness of the elderly as if they were still at the table with children.

Old man sometimes feels sad about being left alone and the past life, but still gains enough strength to live.

인간세상

수많은 가치
수많은 처지
수많은 층위

시끄럽기도 다채롭기도
슬프기도 즐겁기도
미움도 사랑도
싹이 트는 배양토

The human world

Countless values
Numerous situations
Numerous classes of human society

It's noisy and colorful,
sad and happy
It's a potting soil
sprouting for hate and love

시간

무한한 시간의 흐름에
어찌 영원할 수 있는 존재가 있으랴
사람도 정해진 명이 있고 지구와 태양도 때가 되면 그 생을 다하리라

유한한 존재로서 무한의 시간을 감히 이해할 수 있을까마는 나의 마음만은
무색무취로 순화하여 시간의 등에 태워 보내고 싶구나

나도 지우고 인연도 지우고 세상도 다 지워버린 마음이라면,
보이지 않는 바람 같은 시간에 어쩌면 깃털처럼 가볍게 올라탈 수 있지 않
을까…

Time

How can there be something that can last forever in the infinite flow of time?

People also have a certain life

the Earth and the sun will also end their lives when the time comes.

As a limited being, I wonder if I can dare to understand infinite time

but I want to purify my heart into a colorless and odorless thing and send it riding on the back of time.

If I were to erase myself, relationships, and the world,

maybe I can ride on the time like an invisible wind as lightly as a feather⋯

악인의 전성시대

불리한 진실은 묻어버리고
사람들의 관심을 돌리려 선한 사람을 범죄자로 만드는 사람들

가공하고 조작한 사실을 진실인 양 퍼뜨리며 누군가를 죽이는 사람들

결국 진실은 드러나게 마련이라고 믿는 순진한 사람들을 속이며 지배하는 사람들

설마 그 정도까지 악랄할까 고개를 갸웃하는 그대는 바보

The golden age of the Wicked

People who turn good people into criminals to divert attention and conceal
unfavorable truths

People who kill someone by spreading processed and manipulated facts as
if they were the truth

People who dominate society by deceiving innocent people who believe
that the truth will eventually be revealed

You are a fool who tilts your head and wonders if they can be that vicious.

디스토피아

소싯적부터 시험과 경쟁 속에 살아온 사람들
죽을 때까지 우열의 잣대를 품고 사는 사람들
골수까지 박힌 선착순의 악몽
적자생존을 넘어 약육강식의 정글이 된 디스토피아

그러나 이제 한 발짝 떨어져서 바라보자

경쟁은 과정의 놀이가 되어 즐거워야 한다
우열은 배역이 되어 각자의 이야기가 되어야 한다
과정도 배역도 싫으면 관객이 되면 족하다

가족, 친구, 이웃, 동료들과 사랑의 방어선을 구축하자
손에 손 잡은 강강술래로 서로의 구명줄이 되자

종국에는 모두가 평안하자

Dystopia

People who have lived in tests and competition since childhood
People who live with standards of superiority and inferiority until they die
A nightmare of first-come-first-served basis, right down to the bone
A dystopia that goes beyond survival of the fittest and has become a jungle
of the fittest

But now, let's take a step back and look at it

Competition should be enjoyable as a game of process.
Superiority and inferiority must become roles and each person's story.
If you don't like the process or the role, being an audience member is
enough.

Let's build a defense line of love with family, friends, neighbors, and
colleagues.

Let's become each other's lifeline through hand-in-hand Ganggangsul-
lae(traditional Korean circle dance play).

Let's all be at peace in the end

등대

늦은 밤, 신새벽까지
홀로 불을 밝혀 엄마처럼 손짓하는 등대

세상사람 다 욕해도 괜찮다 이리 오너라 손짓하는 엄마

그 마음을 알아주는 선한 이들만이 등대를 사랑한다

바보 같은 등대
엄마 같은 등대

Lighthouse

A lighthouse that lights up alone late at night until the first dawn, beckoning like a mother

Mom beckoning me to come here, saying it's okay for everyone in the world to criticize

Only good people who understand the heart love the lighthouse.

A foolishly kind lighthouse
A lighthouse like a mother

중년아재 1

언제부터인지
슬프거나 억울하거나 잔인한 영화를 한 번에 다 보지 못한다

끊었다가 소화하는 시간이 필요하고 무뎌진 느낌이 들면 이어서 본다
때로는 더 안 보기도 한다

사춘기 소녀들보다 더 연약한 감성의 소유자
나는 이제 중년의 아저씨

Middle-aged man 1

I don't know when it started, but now I can't watch sad, unfair, or cruel movies in one sitting.

If I need time to digest after stopping and become dull, continue watching. Sometimes I don't watch it anymore

Possessor more fragile sensibilities than adolescent girls
I'm now a middle-aged man

늙은 엄마

마음이 허하고 괜스레 종잡을 수 없을 때는 늙은 엄마에게 전화한다

밥은 먹었냐
담배 끊어라
술 좀 줄여라
늦게 다니지 마라

항상 입버릇처럼 하시는 잔소리를 가만히 듣고 알았다며 헤헤거리다 보면
가슴 밑바닥이 온기로 채워진다

듣기 싫었던 그 잔소리가 이제는 내 마지막 방어선이다

My old mother

When I feel empty and can't figure out anything, I call my old mother.

Did you eat well?

Quit smoking

Drink less

Don't go out late

After quietly listening to the nagging that mother always say and then I say, "I see", the bottom of my heart is filled with warmth.

The nagging that I hated hearing is now my last line of defense.

중년아재 2

슬프거나 억울하거나 잔인한 영화를 못 보는 이유로 나이 들어 갑자기 변한 호르몬 탓을 했던 것은 아닐까

이미 삶이 힘들고 지쳐서 굳이 영화로 고통을 더하지 않아도 되거나 감내하지 못하는 것 같다

호르몬의 문제만이 아니라 내가 감당해왔고 지탱해가는 삶 자체가 임계점에 있었던 거다

Middle-aged man 2

I wonder if I blame my hormones for suddenly changing as I get older because I can't watch sad, unfair, or cruel movies.

My life is already difficult enough, so I don't need to add the pain through movies, or I feel like I can't endure the emotional pain caused by such movies.

Not only was it a hormonal problem, but the life I had endured and maintained had reached a critical point.

숙취

연이어 며칠 마신 술로 얼굴이 붓고
라면을 끓여 속을 달래는 아침

창밖의 하늘은 바람도 없이 흐린 흑백인데
휴일이라고 거리엔 사람 대신 배고픈 길고양이만 바쁘다

숙취로 마비된 머리는 별생각이 없어서 세상사 잊고 오히려 편안타

Hangover

This morning, my face was swollen from the alcohol I drank for several days in a row, so I cooked ramyeon to soothe my stomach

The sky outside the window is cloudy gray with no wind
Instead of people, the streets are crowded with hungry stray cats on holidays.

My paralyzed head by a hangover, I don't have any thoughts so I can forget everything in the world and feel at ease.

쉼

사람이 가진 정신의 크기는 정해져 있다

열 개가 들어갈 자리라서 열 한 개가 들어가면 정신이 열한 개로 분산되며 애를 쓴다

열두 개, 열세 개 계속해서 늘어나면 버팅기다가 팽팽해지던 고무줄처럼 끊어진다

열 개가 들어갈 자리를 두세 개는 비워놓고, 또 어느 날엔 모두 비워내고 여유로움과 단순함으로 남겨둬야 한다

그래야 산다

Taking a rest

The size of a person's mind is fixed.

There is room for 10, so when 11 goes in my mind splits into 11 and I struggle.

12 and 13
If it continues to stretch like this, it will hold on and then break like a stretched rubber band.

You should leave 2 or 3 empty spaces where 10 can fit, and one day you should empty them all and leave them with leisure and simplicity.

That's how we can live

인공지능

사람의 정신작용으로 이루어진 세상
도시, 돈, 먹거리, 예술…
사람만이 이뤄내는 세상

사람이 만든 인공지능
지식과 사고와 감성까지 담아 만든 인공지능
인공지능이 다시 녹여내고 섞어서 만드는 새로운 세상

사람이 만든 세상이라고 할 수 있을까?
인공지능 그들이 만든 세상일까?

A.I.

A world made up of human mental processes

City, money, food culture, art···

A world that only people can achieve

Artificial Intelligence created by humans

and created with knowledge, thoughts, and emotions

A new world created by mixing artificial intelligence again

Can we really say that this is a world created by humans?

or, is this a world created by artificial intelligence?

예술의 이해

사진으로 세상을 바라보고
그림으로 세상을 드러내고
음악으로 세상을 표현하고
시로 세상을 노래한다
춤은… 그냥 감정 표출인가… 그건 좀 모르겠네

Understanding of art

Looking at the world through photos

Revealing the world through pictures

Expressing the world through music

Sing the world through poetry

But dancing… is it just an expression of emotion… I'm not sure about that.

주인공

사람들은 세상의 주인공이 되고자 한다
자식들도 세상의 주인공으로 키우려 한다

Boys, be ambitious!
꿈과 이상이라는 말로 부추기며 영생의 왕좌 타이틀처럼 쫓게 한다

그러지 말자
세상의 주인공이라는 것은 없다

내 인생의 주인공일 뿐이다
헛것을 쫓다가 주인공을 못 해서야 쓰나

The main character

People want to be the main characters of the world
They also want to raise their children to become the main character of the world.

"Boys, be ambitious!"
They encourage you with words like dreams and ideals and make you chase after them like the title of the throne of eternal life.

let's not do like that
There is no such thing as being the main character of the world

We are all just the main characters in life

Is it okay if we chase something in vain and fail to become the main character?

잘 산 인생

늙어가며 외롭지 않다는 것은 얘기 상대가 있다는 의미
배우자나 자식들과 일상을 나누기도 하고
친구들과 점심 국수를 먹으며 얘기를 나누고
소주 한잔 걸칠 체력이 있다면 더할 나위 없겠지
인생이 별거 있나
수다 떨 사람이 항상 옆에 있다면 잘 산 인생이지

A good life

Not being lonely as we get older means having someone to talk to
someone who has a good life shares daily life with their spouse and
children
someone who has a good life eats noodles and talks with friends for lunch
Besides, if we have the stamina to drink a glass of Soju
there's nothing better.
Is there anything special in life?
If we always have someone to chat with, it's a life well lived

로드무비

자동차를 타고 어디론가 향해 가며 일어나는 사건들을 담은 영화 로드무비

갈등과 화해,
만남과 헤어짐,
허름한 모텔과 길가 식당,
예기치 않은 사건들,
목적지를 향해 가며 펼쳐지는 스토리의 전개

여행이 끝날 때는 무언가 결론이 나고 등장인물들이 성숙해진다

영화 속 길 위에서의 여정은 인생길의 축소판 같아서 항상 나를 설레게 한다

Road movies

The road movies that contain events that occur while driving a car to somewhere

conflicts and reconciliations

meeting and breakup

Shabby motels and restaurants,

unexpected events,

The storytelling as characters head towards their destination.

At the end of the journey, something comes to a conclusion and the characters mature.

The journey on the road in the movie always excites me because it's like a microcosm of life

겨울병

겨울에 거북이가 되는 사람
목을 움츠려 등딱지 안에 구겨 넣고
봄이 오는 소리를 기다리는 사람

구름 위를 걸어
비바람을 넘고
높은 산을 기어
봄은 오고 있을 테지만

그는 겨우내 앓으며
눈발 날리는 하늘 아래 어딘가를
걷고 또 걸으며
봄소식을 기다린다

쉬 오지 않는 그 봄이 올 때까지
겨울병을 앓는 그를 안고
함께 봄을 기다리는 사람

라일락 향기 나는 길손이
그의 손을 잡고 있다

Winter sickness

A person who becomes a turtle in winter
A person who shrinks his neck and crumples it into his shell and waits for
the sound of spring coming

Spring will be coming
walking on the clouds,
overcoming the wind and rain,
and rawling up a high mountain

He is sick all winter
and walks somewhere under the snowy sky, waiting for the news of
spring.

A person who waits for spring with him,
holding him who is suffering from winter sickness,
until the spring that does not come easily comes.

The lilac-scented traveler is holding his hand.

걷는 이유

걷고 또 걷고 또 걸으면
머릿속, 마음속 장식들이 떨어져 나가고 맨 정신 밑바닥이 드러난다

인생의 암호가 안개 걷히듯 드러난다

건강, 예의, 절제, 중용, 관계, 현재, 의미들…

그래서 매일매일 걸으려고 한다
걷고 또 걸어서 땅바닥 같은 정신의 밑바닥으로 세상을 보게…

Reasons for walking

If I walk and walk and walk again,
the decorations in my head and heart fall away
the bare bottom of mind is revealed.

If I look at the world with a sobriety and bottom of mind, the code of life is
revealed like the fog clears.

Health, manners, moderation, middle path, relationships, present,
meanings…

So I try to walk every day
I walk and walk so that I can see the world from the bottom of mind, which
is like the ground…

내 맘대로 몸관리

어느 날은 술로 몸을 정화합니다

어느 날은 타이레놀을 삼키고 몸을 다스립니다

어느 날은 고되게 걸어봅니다

어느 날은 보이차를 우려내 마십니다

어느 날은 녹용도 먹습니다

어느 날은 채식으로, 어느 날은 고기를 먹어줍니다

지극히 주관적인 땡김에 따라 몸을 잘 관리합니다

Taking care of body the way I want

One day I purify myself with alcohol.

One day, I take Tylenol and control myself.

One day I take a hard walk

One day, I brew some pu-erh tea and drink it.

One day, I even eat deer antler.

Some days I'm a vegetarian, some days I eat meat.

I take good care of my body according to my extremely subjective cravings.

컨슈머 걸

소비를 좋아한다는 여인
소비를 하며 살아있음을 더 느낀다는 여인

다이소부터 티파니 반지까지 사랑하는 물건 폭이 광대역인 여인

가족에게 먹이는 식재료부터 가까운 이들에게 줄 뭔가를 항상 고민하며 농수
산공산품 각종 쇼핑몰 전문가가 된 여인

오늘도 아침부터 커피를 사주는 여인
사랑스러운 자칭 컨슈머 걸

A consumer girl

A woman who likes spending

A woman who feels more alive through consumption

A woman with a wide range of loved items, from Daiso to Tiffany rings.

A woman who has become an expert in various shopping malls for agricultural, fishery, and industrial products, always thinking about things to give to those close to her, from the ingredients she feeds to family.

The woman who buys me coffee this morning again

Lovely self-proclaimed consumer girl

각방

젊을 때는 부부 사이가 안 좋아 각방을 써도 별생각 없었다

나이 들고 각방을 써보니 얼마나 냉랭한 관계인지 알겠다

자다가 가위에 눌리든, 고열로 사경을 헤매든,
심장마비가 와서 고통 속에 저세상으로 가든,
뇌출혈이 와서 죽거나 반신불수가 되든 상관 안 하겠다는 표현이 각방 쓰는
거더라

늙어가는 사람들이여
각방은 위험하다

Sleeping in separated rooms

When I was younger, I didn't think much even though our relationship was so bad that we had to sleep in separate rooms.

As I got older and sleep in separate rooms, I realized how growing apart the relationship was.

The expression of sleeping in separated rooms means that my spouse won't care if I suffer from sleep paralysis, feel like dying due to high fever or heart attack and part hence in pain, or have a cerebral hemorrhage and die or become paralyzed.

People who are getting old! Sleeping in separated rooms is dangerous for you

숨바꼭질

외부적으로 사람들 속에서 소모되고
내적으로도 지치고 소진되어 버린 밤

내성적인 나는 숨을 곳이 필요하다

사춘기 시절엔 내성적인 성격이 콤플렉스 같아 책 속에 숨어 살았고
다 커서는 사람과 일에 치여 여전히 또 숨을 데를 찾고 있다

생각해보니 어릴 때도 숨바꼭질이 제일 잼있었어!

Hide and seek

A night when I was consumed externally among people,
tired and exhausted internally

I'm an introvert so I need a place to hide.

When I was a teenager, I had a complex about my introverted personality,
so I hid in books.
When I grow up, I'm overwhelmed by people and work and am still
looking for a place to hide.

Now that I think about it, even when I was young, hide and seek was the
most fun I had!

사량꾼

친근한 A가 좋았다

달려드는 B도 싫지는 않았다

다 좋은데 A는 확 땡겨오질 않았고, B는 살짝 거부감이 있었다

뭔가 확실한 연애가 아니었다

둘 사이에서 긴가민가 오랫동안 방황했다

슬슬 지쳐갈 무렵 C가 나타났다

그래! C를 잡아보자

A, B는 일단 놔두고 C가 어떤지 새로운 사냥을 해보는 거야

안 되면 마는 거지

나는야 사랑을 사냥하는 사량꾼

Love hunter

I liked the friendly A

and I didn't dislike B approaching me either.

It's all good, but A wasn't really into it, and B was a bit reluctant.

It wasn't really a romantic relationship.

I wandered between the two for a long time.

When I was getting tired, C appeared.

okay! Let's catch C

Let's leave A and B alone for now and try a new hunt to see what C is like.

If it doesn't work, I'm done.

I'm a love hunter who hunts for love

어느 도시

유채화 같은 밤하늘
맑게 깜박이는 빌딩의 옥상 신호등
도로가 점점이 불 밝힌 가로등
도시를 가로지르는 검은 강

언젠가 본 듯한 열대의 남국 어느 도시 모습

한밤에 홀로 깨어 바라보는 베란다 창밖의 이국적인 풍경

술에 취하지 않은 정신이 오랜만이어선가
내가 사는 동네가 이국적으로 바뀐 건가

A city

A night sky like an oil painting

A traffic lights on the roof of a building flashing clearly

Street lights dotted along the road

Black river running through the city

A city in a tropical southern country that seems like something I've seen before

I woke up alone in the middle of the night, looking at the exotic scenery outside the veranda window

Is it because it's been a while since I've been sober,

or has the neighborhood I live in become exotic?

이별

지나고 보니 잘 맞았던 사이는 아니었어
그래도 그냥 좋았지 서로가 '너'뿐이었거든

지금은 식어버렸지만 가끔 생각나네
식었다 해도 차가운 건 아니야 그냥 열기를 잃은 거지

새로운 사람도 나타났어
그 사람 때문에 우리 관계가 끝난 건 아니지만 쉽게 정리될 수 있었던 건 사
실이야

잘 지내면 되는 거야, 각자가…

Breakup

In hindsight, we weren't a good couple

But it's just good because there was only 'you' for each other.

It's gone cold now, but I think of it sometimes.

Even if it cools down, it doesn't mean it's very cold. It just loses heat of love.

A new person also appeared

Our relationship didn't end because of it, but it's true it could have been easily resolved.

just needs to get along well··· each person···

최우수상

오전 세시 반
속이 불편해 잠 깨어 창을 열고 담배를 물었다

인적도 차도 끊긴 텅 빈 도로
건너편 아파트 앞 길가에 어둠 사이로 하얀 패딩 입은 사람이
걷다가 말다가 서 있다가 걷는 모습이 보인다

마약이 퍼졌다더니 약에 취하면 저리 걷나?

내가 사는 아파트 쪽으로 점점 가까워지면서 강아지 한 마리 더 보이고…
아… 저 강아지가 얼마나 보챘으면 이 한밤에 산책을 나왔을까

뭔가 상을 만들어 줘야 될 거 같다
전에 없던 새로운 열녀효부, 개노예 최우수상!

Grand Prize

A.M. 3:30,

I woke up feeling uncomfortable and opened the window, smoked a cigarette.

An empty road with no people or cars
on the street in front of the apartment across the street, a person wearing white padded jacket appears in the darkness.
I see him walking and then standing and then, and walking.

They say drugs are spreading among people, do people walk like that when they are high on drugs?

As I get closer to the apartment where I live, I see another dog···
Ah··· how fussy that puppy must have been to go for a walk in the middle of the night?

I think that I should make some kind of award.
The grand prize in the 'Slave of dog' category is awarded to a new virtuous and filial wife who has never been seen before!

밤 술, 낮 차 1

밤 술, 낮 차의 시간들
안으로 안으로 들어가는 시간들
추위도 싫고 세상도 지쳐
숨어드는 시간들

연약한 인간의 피부가 자연 속에서는 버겁듯이
연약한 나의 마음도 세상 속에서 버겁다

옷을 입어 보호막을 치듯
내 마음에도 무언가 필요하다

밤 술, 낮 차… 내 마음의 거위털 패딩

Drinking at night, tea during the day 1

Time of drinking at night, tea during the day
Time to go deeper inside
Time to hide because I don't like the cold and I'm tired of the world

Just as fragile human skin is burdensome in nature,
even my weak heart feels burdened in this world.

As if putting on clothes to create a protective shield
I need something in my heart too

Drinking at night, chilling with tea during the day… is the padded jacket of
my heart

3의 위엄

십만 원이 아쉬운 사람에게 이십만 원은 여유를 부릴 수 있고
삼십만 원은 부자가 되게 한다

배고픈 사람에게 빵 한 개는 간에 기별이 안 가고
빵 두 개 정도 돼야 감사하다
빵이 세 개라면 주위에 베풀 수 있는 신이 내린 빵이 된다

그래서 3은 강력함을 넘어 신성을 가진다.

Majesty of 3

For those who feel the lack with 100,000 won, they can afford with 200,000 won
and 300,000 won makes them rich

One of bread doesn't go a long way to a hungry person.
If the person had 2 loaves of bread, it would be thankful
If the person has 3 loaves, they become God-given bread that you can give to people around.

So 3 has a divinity that goes beyond strength.

MBTI가 F인 사람

조그만 일에 슬프다
조그만 일도 무시하고 배려하지 못하니 슬픈 거다
속 좁다 욕하지 마라
조그만 거도 챙기는 사람이라 조그만 거 무시하면 슬프다

People whose MBTI is F

They feel sad over small things

It's sad that ignored small things and can't be considered.

Don't criticize me for being narrow-minded.

I'm a person who takes care of even the smallest things, so it's sad when I'm
ignored those little things.

어쩌다 마주친 슬픔

돼지불백을 먹는데
뼛조각 같은 것이 씹혔다
갈비도 아닌데 웬 뼛조각일까…
이가 상할까 조심히 뱉어 살펴보니 돼지뼈 같지가 않다.
하얀 조각
조그맣게 깨져 나간 내 이빨…

The sadness I encountered by chance

When I was eating pork belly, something that looked like a piece of bone
chewed on.
It's not even ribs, so why are they bone pieces?
I spit it out carefully to avoid damaging my teeth, and when I looked at it, it
didn't look like pork bone.
It's white pieces that my tooth was slightly broken…

늦게 안 두려움

약하기 때문에 화장으로 현혹하려 하고
웃음과 애교로 비집고 들어온다

약하기 때문에 독해지고 용의주도해지며
궁극적으로 악해질 수 있다

하여 나는 갈수록 여자가 무섭다

나와 자식들의 일상에 태풍과 엄동설한을 몰고 다니는
우리 집 여자는 더 무섭다

A fear I found out late

Because they are weak, they try to deceive them with makeup.
and coming in with laughter and cuteness

Because they are weak, they become poisonous and suspicious.
even they can ultimately become evil

I'm increasingly scared of women
The woman in my house who is bringing typhoons and severe winter cold
into my and my children's daily lives scares me more

호모 스토리우스

소설, 영화, 만화만 이야기랴
커피숍 가득 메운 수다 소리
길 걸으며 전화하고 문자하고…
넘치고 넘치는 이야기들
이야기 소리에 지쳐서 찾은 골방
또 이렇게 쓰는 나만의 이야기

Homo storius(The human species with stories)

Are novels, movies, and comics the only stories?
The sound of chatter filled the coffee shop
Calling and texting while walking down the street…
Overflowing stories
A small room I found after getting tired of hearing stories.
My own story that I'm writing like this again

밤 술, 낮 차 2

버겁고 지친 삶이 싫어
종종 안으로 숨어드는 사람

하지만 결국은
더욱 깊고 성숙해져 또 돌아오고야 마는 사람

삶의 의미 그 이상으로 삶을 깊게 사는 사람

오랜 시간 찻물이 은근히 배어
찻잎 색이 되어 버린 백자찻잔처럼
스며들 듯이 세상의 일부가 되었지만
또 철저히 이방인인 사람
조용히 지켜봐주기만 하면 되는 사람

숨어드는 그 시간을 기다려주기만 하면 되는 사람

세상에 소비되는 그 사람은
점점 소진되지만
곁을 지켜주는 사랑하는 누군가는 가진 사람

Drinking at night, tea during the day 2

A person who often hides inside because the person hates a burdensome and tiring life

But in the end, the person becomes deeper and more mature and comes back again

A person who lives life deeply beyond its meaning

A person who has become a part of the world, like a white porcelain teacup that has been subtly soaked with tea over a long period of time and turned the color of tea leaves, but is also a complete stranger.
A person who just needs to quietly watch

A person who just needs to wait for the time to hide

The person who is consumed by the world is gradually exhausted, but has someone who loves and protects their side

중성

설거지에 쓰는 중성세제
복부비만의 원인 중성지방
울 고양이는 중성화수술
60줄 돼가는 나도 중성인간

Neutrality

Neutral detergent used for washing dishes

Neutral fat, the cause of abdominal obesity

My cat has been neutered surgery

I who am almost 60-year-old also an intersex person.

그냥 살기

나라는 인간
세상이 만들어낸 인간
내 탓이 어디 있으리
유전자도 성향도 기질도 현재의 모습도 세상의 산물
나무도 개미도 사자도 그렇고…
그러니 고민 말고 생긴 대로 살아가자

Just living

I'm a human being
human being created by the world
Maybe it's not my fault
Genes, tendencies, temperament, and current appearance are all products
of the world.
Trees, ants, lions, etc…
So, let's not worry and just live the way we are.

미워할 상대

퇴근길 반주로는 삭여지지 않는 울분
우리는 누군가 미워할 상대가 필요하다

정치인 미워하기는 손해다
아무리 미워해도 반질한 가면 쓴 얼굴로 반사시키니
내 화만 커진다

그래서 미워하면 주눅 드는
스포츠스타, 연예인이 공공연히 미움의 대상이 된다
그들은 당장 광고가 끊기고 잘못했다고 고개를 숙인다

그래, 우리의 승리다!
오랜만에 만끽하는 작은 승리

Someone to hate

Anger that cannot be alleviated by drinking with supper on the way home
from work
So we need someone to hate

It's a loss to hate politicians
No matter how much I hate them, my anger only grows because they
reflect it back with a polished masked face.

So sports stars, celebrities who become intimidated when they are hated
they often become an object of public hatred.
They immediately cut off the commercial and bow their heads saying they
did something wrong.

Yes, it's our victory! A small victory that we can enjoy after a long time.

자기 합리화

금요일 오후
노곤하다

일주일의 밥벌이에 지쳐서라고 당당하게 말하고 싶지만…

매일 이어진 퇴근길 소주가 원인 같아서 좀 찔린다

아니야, 소주가 없었으면 못 버텼어
암만 그렇고말고…

Self-justification

I'm exhausted on friday afternoon

I want to confidently say that I'm tired of earning a living for a week, but…

but I feel guilty because the soju I drink on my way home from work every
day is the cause of my fatigue.

Nope, I couldn't have survived without Soju.
Of course that's right…!!

만 보 걷기

살기 위해서 걷는다는 말이 맞습니다
잦은 술에 죽을 거 같아서 걷습니다
술을 먹기 위해 걷는 것이 아닙니다

우선 살아야 합니다
그래야 술이 들어갑니다
그래야 이 생을 버텨냅니다

Walking 10,000 steps

It's true that we walk to live.
I walk because I feel like I'm going to die from frequent drinking.
not because to drink

I have to live first
that's how alcohol goes in
and that's how I endure this life

거짓말

절대권력자 왕은 거짓말을 하지 않는다
세상이 발아래이니 거짓말이 필요치 않다

거짓말은 왕 바로 아랫사람부터 시작하여 밑바닥 힘없는 사람들 차지다.
살아남기 위한 방패 같은 거짓말이 짠하고 이해된다

하지만 나 살자고 남을 죽이는 거짓말은 칼이고 총이다
인간세상에서 감싸주지 못한다

오늘 너의 거짓말은 마음은 아프지만 선을 넘지는 않았다

Lie

A king who has absolute power doesn't lie

because there is no need to lie when the world is at his feet.

Lies are spread to the most powerless people, starting from those just below

the king.

The lies that act as a shield to survive are heartbreaking and understandable.

But the lie that kills others for my own life is a sword and a gun.

The human world cannot protect.

Your lies today hurt my heart, but you didn't cross the line.

허벅지

나이 들며 초라해지는 허벅지였습니다
심기일전! 이래 살면 안 된다는 절박함이 걷게 만들었습니다
요새 많이 걷습니다
어느덧 허벅지가 볼 만합니다
얼굴이 아니라 허벅지를 보고 뿌듯함에 잠깁니다
나르시스트가 아니라 허벅지스트입니다

Thigh

It's a thigh that became shabby as I got older.

but let's do my best!

The desperation that I couldn't continue living like this made me walk.

I walk a lot these days

so now, my thighs are in good shape

I feel proud when I see my thighs, not my face.

It's not a narcissist,

it's a thighist.

크싼티페

소크라테스의 악처 크싼티페를 아시오?

무일푼, 날건달 같은 밥벌이 무관심남 소크라테스를 대신해
가장으로 가정을 지켜낸 악바리 여성

서양판 평강공주 같은 억척녀 크싼티페
그녀는 결국 세상에 남는 철학자를 길러냈다

우리 집 여자는 과연…
철학자를 낼 것인가, 술꾼을 낼 것인가

Xanthipe

Do you know Xanthipe, the evil wife of Socrates?

An evil woman who protected her family as the head of the household head in place of Socrates, a penniless, gangster-like man with no interest in earning a living.

Xanthipe is a strong woman who looks like the Western version of Princess Pyeonggang

She ultimately raised a philosopher who will remain in the world.

Will the woman in my house⋯ raise a philosopher
or raise a drinker?

공공근로

날이 풀리고 제법 푸근해졌습니다
팔순 어머니 애타게 기다리시던 공공근로가 시작됐네요
개나리꽃 고운 단체복을 입으시고 봄맞이하시니 기분 좋으신가 봅니다
일하며 친구분들도 만나시고 늘그막 돈벌이에 당당해지신 울 어머니
웬일로 점심도 사드시고 귀가하십니다
복된근로로 이름을 바꾸어야겠습니다

Public job

The day has cleared up and it has become quite warm.

The public job that my 80-year-old mother has been anxiously awaiting for has begun.

I guess she feels good about welcoming spring wearing the pretty forsythia flower uniform.

My mother met friends while working and became proud of making money as she got older.

She bought lunch and ate it before returning home

It should be renamed public job as Blessed job.

Q&A

물어보는 자
추궁하는 자
거짓말하지 말라고 하는 자
사실인지 확인하는 자
물어볼 힘을 가진 자

대답해야 하는 자
기억나지 않아 힘들어하는 자
대답을 찾느라 땀을 내는 자
침묵하면 잘못될까 겁내는 자

묻고 답하는 것이 무서운 곳이 많더라

Q&A

The one who asks,

the one who interrogates,

the one who tells you not to lie

the one who checks if it is true

the one who have the power to ask

the one who must answer

the one who has a hard time because they can't remember

the one who is nervous to find the answer

the one who is afraid that something will go wrong if they keep silent

There are many places where asking and answering questions is scary.

바벨탑

창밖으로 전에 없던 높은 건물이 하늘을 나눈다
신에 대한 도전으로 여겼던 바벨탑이 뚝딱 생기는 시대

인간의 오랜 노동과 저축이 쌓여 이룩한 자본으로
우뚝 선 건물
무에서 유로 나타난 건물

창조는 이제 인간도 제법 한다

The Tower of Babel

Outside the window, a tall building like never before divides the sky.
An era in which the Tower of Babel, which was considered a challenge to
God, was built quickly.

A building that stands tall as capital built from long years of human labor
and savings.
A building that came from nothing

Now humans are also quite creative.

모닝커피

미처 나를 챙기지 못하여 몸도 마음도 내가 아닌 듯한 아침

부담스러운 일들이 쌓인
사무실에 들어가기 버거워 커피로 아침을 깨운다

그래, 비즈니스맨은 이런 거지
내가 밭 갈러 가는 건 아니잖아
커피 쫌 분위기 있게 먹어볼까

후루룩 촵촵…
숭늉 마시듯 들이키는 직장인의 폼 안 나는 모닝커피

Morning coffee

A morning where I feel like I'm not myself in body or mind because I'm not
able to take care of myself.

It's hard to go into the office that burdensome things piled up,
so the morning coffee wake me up.

Yeah, this is what business men are like.
I'm not going to plow the field.
Let's try some coffee in a nice atmosphere.

Slurp, slurp like drinking Sungnyung(scorched-rice water)
It's not-so-fantastic morning coffee of an business man

욕

욕이 나오는 상황
욕먹어도 싼 인간들
욕을 참아서 복장 터지는 사람

욕은 상식이어라
불법과 합법이 아니라, 사람이냐 짐승이냐의 선에서 욕이 터져 나온다

맘껏 욕해야 한다
참으면 세상이 병든다

Swear words

A situation where swearing occurs
People who deserve to be criticized
A person who endures swearing and loses his clothes

Swearing is common sense
and erupts not on the line between illegal and legal,
but between human and animal.

You must curse as much as you like
If you hold back, the world will get sick.

구례의 봄

길 위에 하얀 벚꽃이 흘렁거리고
배 밭에는 이화가 하얗게 강건하다

천지 빛깔이 하얘 몽롱한데
섬진강은 온통 은빛으로 반짝여서 이내 이승의 풍광이 아니다

십여 년이 지나도록 도시에서 봄을 맞는 내 머릿속에
여전히 구례의 봄이 가득하다

Spring in Goo-rye

White cherry blossoms are fluttering on the road
Pear blossoms are white and strong in the pear field.

The colors of the sky and the earth are white and hazy
The Seomjin River is all sparkling with silver, and it soon becomes an out-of-this-world scenery.

More than 10years later, in my mind as I welcome spring in the city,
my mind is still full of Goorye's spring.

봄이 좋은 이유

이젠 봄인가 보오
꽃들도 슬금슬금 피고 있지만
내 맘이 더 활짝 피고 있소

추위와 세상살이 고통이 비슷한 통증이라서
그중 하나가 사라지니 살 것 같소

그래서 이 봄이 너무 좋소

The reason why I love spring

I guess it's spring now
Even though the flowers are slowly blooming
my heart is blooming more brightly

The pain of cold and life are similar,
I guess I will be able to survive because one of them has gone.

That's why I love this spring so much

호모 스토리우스

ⓒ 신 훈, 2024

초판 1쇄 발행 2024년 5월 10일

지은이	신 훈
펴낸이	이기봉
편집	좋은땅 편집팀
펴낸곳	도서출판 좋은땅
주소	서울특별시 마포구 양화로12길 26 지월드빌딩 (서교동 395-7)
전화	02)374-8616~7
팩스	02)374-8614
이메일	gworldbook@naver.com
홈페이지	www.g-world.co.kr

ISBN 979-11-388-3131-4 (03810)